Bodyguard SEAL

SEALs of Coronado

PAIGE TYLER

Editing by Jennifer Jakes / The Killion Group, Inc.

Copyediting by RVP Editing

Bodyguard SEAL

PROLOGUE

Sana'a, Yemen

"EVERYTHING LOOKS GOOD ON THIS SIDE," PETTY Officer First Class, Noah Bradley, murmured into his mic as he surveyed the industrial building across the street through his night vision scope, noting the three people moving around the enclosed compound. "No indication they're aware we're here."

Half a dozen different voices called out confirmation over the radio, but fellow SEAL Teammate Chief Chasen Ward was the only one he recognized. Another indication of how big of a goat rope this damn operation had turned into over the course of the past two days. Talk about too many cooks spoiling the broth. He just prayed things went smoothly.

Noah ignored the background chatter of other people calling out their location as they moved into support positions around the large square building he and everyone else would be entering in a few minutes. He couldn't help but notice the ridiculous amount of unnecessary babble. As far as radio communication went, Noah and his Teammates only spoke to each other once to start the entry and then not again until the shit hit the fan. Clearly, all the nonstandard players involved in this operation didn't like to do the same.

He let out a snort as he flipped his night vision goggles back down.

Nonstandard players was a good way to describe Interpol and the U.S. Department of Treasury. Okay, maybe that wasn't fair. Interpol *did* occasionally take part in various international law enforcement operations, but the Treasury Department? Hell, he didn't even realize their agents owned tactical equipment. Then again, everything about this operation was unusual, so why not the people involved?

This mission was merely one part of a bigger world-wide effort with fourteen raids going off around the globe, all synchronized to happen at the exact same moment, so the bad guys wouldn't be able to warn each other what was coming. The objective? Taking down the largest terrorist funding organization in existence. The location they were at here in Yemen was supposedly pumping somewhere in the neighborhood of a hundred million dollars a year into various terrorist operations around the globe. Toss in the other ones throughout Eastern Europe, Asian, Africa, and South America and you were talking billions. With a capital "B."

The crazy thing was that according to the intel they'd gotten, Noah and his Teammates weren't likely to find the two things terrorists liked to fund their operations with—drugs and human trafficking—in this raid. Instead, these bad guys made their money through pirating bootleg downloads of music, movies, and books, along with mountains of knockoff Air Jordans, Gucci handbags, and iPhones.

Noah had to admit that books and purses weren't exactly the first things that popped into his head when he thought of piracy, but apparently both were huge in the world of terrorism.

"No sign of Magpie," someone announced over the radio in his earpiece.

Magpie was the code name for the financier who allegedly led the world-wide piracy operation. No one knew the guy's real name, or even where he was from. Just that he was some kind of international businessman, rich in his own right, and apparently in the habit of collecting pretty, shiny things. Hence the bizarre nickname.

Magpie was supposed to be here tonight, which was part of the reason they'd waited to raid the place until now and not gone in when they'd gotten into the country three days ago. The possibility of capturing the man pulling the strings would be a huge win for the good guys, not only taking billions out of the terrorist coffers, but also giving them the person who'd practically written the book on funding terrorist operations around the world.

"Entry team, this is Alpha Lead," a voice said over the radio, intruding on his thoughts. "We're not waiting any longer for Magpie and have gotten the clearance to move. World-wide go is in two minutes."

Noah bit his tongue to stop himself from cursing out loud. Glenn Woods was the senior Treasury Department agent on this operation. Sometimes, he came across as okay, but other times—like now—he seemed pompous as all hell. *Alpha Lead*? WTF?

He was still thinking about that when he heard Chasen call out that the entry team was on the move. Noah immediately pushed the button on the mic, signaling he heard the command. Four more clicks quickly followed as Sam Travers, Wes Marshall, and Lane Robbins, the recent transfer from one of the other platoons in SEAL Team 5, all responded.

Noah slipped over the parapet that encircled the roof he'd been perched atop for the past few fours, sliding down the rope he'd left hanging there earlier. Sticking to the shadows, he swiftly moved across the street to the mud and brick wall that surrounded the compound, heading toward the low section along the back that he'd identified as his entry point when the mission had first gotten the green light.

As he ran along the base of the rough stone wall, Noah found himself subconsciously paying attention to his left knee, mindful of even the slightest twinge of pain or weakness. He let out a little sigh of relief as he realized it felt good... solid. Not that it shouldn't have. It'd been nearly two months since the mission in Nigeria when he'd gotten slightly blown up and failed to stick the landing properly, ending up with a grade 2 ligament sprain to both the MCL and ACL. Nothing too serious, but nothing to laugh at, either.

Truthfully, his messed-up knee was the reason there were five SEALs on this mission instead of the four they would have normally sent. Headquarters wanted another person on the mission in case things didn't go as planned. It wasn't merely concern that his knee would give out at the wrong moment. Noah was smart enough to know HQ was nervous about how he'd respond under fire after almost getting killed. He couldn't blame them. Hell, he hadn't done anything more than low intensity training in two months. They needed a back-up plan if he mentally checked out.

Noah was over the wall and pulling the silenced M4 off his back in one smooth motion. Dropping to a knee, he locked and loaded a round in the chamber, then clicked his mic one time. When four other clicks followed, he was up and moving for his designated entry point—a window on the southeast corner of the building.

There were more guards patrolling the compound than he'd seen from the rooftop across the street a few minutes ago, but he only had to engage with one of them as he transversed the shadowy space between the wall and the building. He and the bad guy spotted each other at exactly the same time, but Noah was faster getting his weapon up and the guard hit the ground with little more than a grunt and a thud.

M4 in hand, Noah ran the rest of the way to the building. The window squeaked a little when he opened it and he held his breath, sure more guards would come running. But when nothing but silence continued to fill the thick night air, he hopped up on the window ledge and slipped inside.

He scanned the place with his NVGs, realizing he was in a storage room. The large space was lined with heavy steel shelving loaded to the ceiling with hundreds of boxes. The writing on the side of the boxes didn't mean anything to him. Shoes, maybe?

Noah quickly moved over to the door, opening it a fraction of an inch and peeking out. He cursed when the lenses of his NVGs flared so brightly it nearly blinded him thanks to the light in the room on the other side of it saturating them. Reaching up, he flipped them up so they locked back against his tactical helmet.

Making sure the coast was clear, he stepped out of the storage room and into the main part of the building. It was stuffed with more shelving units and while he could hear voices all around him, the heavily loaded shelves blocked his view and made it impossible to know for sure exactly how many bad guys they were going to have to deal with.

Plans for these types of operations tended to be basic. No need to get too complicated when everything went to shit once the shooting started. But the concept he and Chasen had worked out was that Noah would get inside the building first and find a position that'd allow him to see as much of the building as possible—preferably from someplace high up—where he could cover his Teammates when they came in.

Noah scanned the room for options, locking in on the rough metal stairs leading to the second level. It overlooked the main floor and would give him a great vantage point to keep an eye on things. He carefully headed in that direction, praying no one saw him. Luckily, no one did.

The second floor was dark and while there were a few crates and pallets of cardboard boxes here and there, there weren't any bad guys in sight. He slipped between two of the crates near the railing overlooking the first floor, wedging himself forward on his stomach until he had a good view of the area below him.

From here, Noah could see that the lower level was the size of a basketball court with half a dozen long tables lined up down the middle surrounded by all those shelves. Computers covered two of the tables while electronic gear he couldn't hope to identify occupied two more, and a mountain of pristine looking smart phones took up the rest. Ten men packaged up the phones in boxes that didn't look much different than something you'd find at an Apple store. Damn, the whole operation was way more high-tech than he'd envisioned, that was for sure.

Nearly fifteen additional people moved amongst the shelves, some pulling boxes down, others loading them on. Most of them were armed with guns, which was a hell of a lot more than Interpol and the Treasury intel had implied would be here.

Why was he not really shocked?

"I'm in overwatch position on the second floor, south end," Noah murmured into his mic. "Approximately twenty-five people in all, ten carrying pistols and four with AK-47s. I'll take the guys with the rifles when the shooting starts."

Chasen, Sam, Wes, and Lane all confirmed with single clicks.

"Any sign of Magpie?" Agent Woods murmured.

"Negative," Noah replied.

True, he didn't know what the guy looked like, but seriously, no one down there looked like a rich, powerful terrorist financier.

Thirty seconds later, he caught sight of movement in the far reaches of the warehouse. His Teammates were moving into position. Lane took the first armed man down without firing a shot, slipping up behind the guy among the shelves and dragging him down without a sound. But then the shooting started, and Noah didn't have time to think about anything other than lining up his weapon's optical sights on targets and pulling the trigger.

He focused on dealing with the four men armed with assault rifles first, then kept an eye out for anyone sneaking through the shelving units. He was so intent on that he didn't notice someone coming at him from the right until he heard the sound of boots on the wood floor.

Rolling over onto his back was impossible in the narrow space between the two crates. Getting his M4 around was even less of an option. But he got flipped over far enough onto his side to reach for the SIG 9mm holstered on his right thigh just as a man carrying an AK-47 came into view, the barrel of the weapon already pointing at Noah's face.

Knowing he wouldn't have time to draw his gun, he kicked out with his right leg, catching the man in the knee with the heel of his boot as the guy pulled the trigger.

The man wailed in pain and tumbled forward, a hail of bullets hitting the crates on either side of Noah, one into the floor a mere inch from his right ear, and another into the center of his tactical vest. Even with the ceramic plate to protect him, at this range, the heavy 7.62mm round impacted with the force of a mule kick and it felt like something had stomped his chest flat.

He was still wondering if his lungs would ever work again when the man landed on top of him. Noah decided that breathing could wait.

As they fought over control of the assault rifle, Noah tried to reach down with one hand for his SIG. That nearly got his face shot off as the damn AK-47 went off twice scant inches from his head. Ears ringing like crazy, he gave up going for his pistol and instead focused on getting a hand around the still warm barrel of the man's weapon.

Getting a good grip, he slammed it into the guy's face half a down times, breaking his nose.

He'd hoped the blows would knock the man senseless—or at least rattle him enough so that Noah could end the fight—but the asshole kept fighting. They were both kicking and punching so hard that the crates to either side almost toppled over on them. The man simply wouldn't go down.

A vicious punch in the throat had Noah reeling back, choking and fighting once again for air. The man slammed into Noah, driving him back toward the railing overlooking the lower level, going for the SIG holstered on Noah's thigh at the same time.

Shit.

Knowing he had about half a second before the guy put holes through all his important parts, Noah did the only thing he could. He latched onto the other man's shoulders, dragging the guy with him as he felt himself go over the railing.

Noah twisted his body as he fell, hoping he'd be able to use the other man's body to absorb the impact. The bad guy's back slammed into the top of a metal shelf, but the relief was short lived as they both bounced off and started to tumble again. For a moment, Noah was sure he was going to hit the floor head first, but somehow, he landed on his feet. He had a split second to silently cheer before the man landed on his left leg. Pain spiked through the side of Noah's knee like a red-hot poker and he immediately went down, biting his tongue to keep from screaming in agony.

Gritting his teeth, he drew his pistol and rolled over, expecting to see the guy who'd fallen on him climbing to his feet, ready to charge at him again. But one look confirmed that wasn't going to be a problem. Somehow, the man ended up in even worse shape than Noah. He was lying on the floor unmoving, his head bent sideways at a weird angle, blood coming out of his ears and nose.

Noah winced as he clambered to his feet, forcing himself to ignore the throbbing in his leg as he stumbled through the aisle between the other shelving units, looking for the next threat.

He reached the center of the big warehouse and the long lines of tables when he realized the shooting had stopped. A few seconds later, Chasen calling out, *All Clear* over the radio. Noah's earpiece immediately filled with chatter as the Interpol and Treasury agents moved in. Leaning against one of the shelves, he took the weight off his left leg and breathed in one long sigh of relief as the throbbing eased a little. The loose, floppy feeling in the knee joint was even worse than the pain. He'd torn the ligaments for sure.

The thought of what that might mean for him and his future in the SEALs made his head spin so much he almost didn't hear Chasen asking over the radio if he was okay. It took a moment to figure out what to say.

"Yeah, I'm good," he finally replied. "No problem at all."

Agent Woods didn't even try to hide how excited he was as he moved around the long row of tables, going through all the crap they'd confiscated in the raid. Noah had to admit, he was pretty stoked as well. While the boxes stuffed with knock-off Air Jordans, Jimmy Choo heels, and Hermes handbags were one thing, it was the computer servers full of bootlegs books and music that was where the real money was at.

"Combine this stuff with what the other teams took in around the world tonight and in one fell swoop, we've yanked a billion dollar's worth of funding out of terrorist hands," Wood said. "This is going to bring their current operations to its knees."

"I'd be a lot happier if one of the teams managed to capture Magpie," Chasen muttered, brushing Noah's shoulder slightly as he stepped between him and Wes to stand near the table. His blue eyes narrowed. "With him still around, they'll almost certainly find a way to recoup their losses. Probably a lot sooner than we'd like."

Noah would have agreed if he wasn't so busy clenching his jaw to keep from groaning in agony. Chasen's accidental bump against his shoulder had nudged him off balance just enough to force him to take a step sideways, making his knee throb all over again. His heart thumped faster as a cold sweat hit him and his vision blurred.

Do not pass out.

If smashing his face against the floor didn't kill him, the embarrassment damn well would.

Out of the corner of his eye, Noah saw Wes and Sam looking at him in obvious concern. A quick look Lane's way told him that his other Teammate was equally worried.

Oh, hell. They know something is up.

"What's wrong?" Wes whispered, looking at him in confusion.

Noah opened his mouth with every intention of lying his ass off and say nothing was wrong, but then the pain in his knee flared again and he almost fell over. Wes was immediately at his side even as Lane appeared at the other, both reaching out to keep him from going down. He quickly waved them off, darting a quick look at Chasen to see if his chief had seen. Fortunately, Chasen was too busy talking to Woods to notice.

One look at his Teammates convinced Noah there was no way they were going to let this go. He grimaced. "I think I screwed something up in my knee when I fell from the second floor. I'm hoping if I can get back to the hotel and put ice on, it'll be okay. But if Chasen finds out, I'm toast."

It was obvious from their expressions that his buddies thought he was being stupid. And yeah, maybe he was. But the hell he'd gone through while on limited duty over the past two months was something he never wanted to deal with again. Fortunately, Wes, Sam, and Lane seemed willing to go along with his plea for help, which was good enough for now.

Lane casually moved closer to his left, giving Noah a shoulder to lean on so he could take weight off his bum knee, while Wes and Sam moved in front of them so Chasen wouldn't be able to see anything if he happened to look his way.

By the time everyone was done talking, Noah was wiped out. While Chasen and Woods talked endlessly, he stood there dreaming of burying his whole leg in a mountain of ice, then keeping it there until he couldn't feel a damn thing.

Noah's plan was to hang out until Chasen and the other people left. Then he'd hobble his ass out to one of the Land Rovers and get the hell out of there. If he was lucky, he'd have a full eight hours to nurse his knee back to health before he and his Team had to board a plane home.

Unfortunately, Chasen didn't leave with everyone else. Instead, he leaned back against the table, casually regarding Noah and his Teammates. Noah quickly straightened up, putting a little distance between him and Lane.

"Noah, could I talk to you for a minute?" Chasen looked pointedly at the rest of the guys. "Alone."

Crap. So much for hiding this from his chief.

When Wes, Lane, and Sam hesitated, Noah gave them a slight nod. After a moment, they walked out of the building, but not before glancing back at him nervously.

"What's up, Chief?" Noah asked, trying to sound chill even as he did everything he could to keep weight off his left leg.

Chasen pinned him with a look that was all too knowing. "How bad is it?"

Noah's gut clenched. "What do you mean?"

The chief frowned. "I heard the damn thud when you hit the floor from all the way across the warehouse and I've seen the way you've been babying your left leg, so stop screwing around and tell me how bad the knee is."

Noah sighed. What was the point? It wasn't like he'd be able to hide it from Chasen forever. "I don't know how bad it is. That asshole I was fighting landed right on my leg. I'm worried I may have ripped my whole damn knee apart."

Chasen let out a curse. "And you didn't think this was something you should tell me?"

"I was worried about what headquarters would do if they found out I hurt my knee again," Noah admitted. "The doctor was already talking about a medical discharge if it didn't respond to limited duty and physical therapy. And that was *before* some dumb bastard fell on it."

Chasen didn't say anything, instead getting on the radio to call in the medic who'd come with them in case anyone got injured. A few minutes later, a jackass of a man with a shitty bedside manner was prodding and yanking on Noah's leg like it was a stuffed toy he was trying to steal from the county fair.

"I'm no doctor, but I've seen this kind of injury a lot," the blond man finally said. "The ACL and MCL are most likely only sprained and torn, so you can probably avoid surgery if you stay off the leg for a while."

Dammit.

"Define a while," Chasen said.

The medic shrugged as he glanced at the chief. "Sixty days, maybe. He'll need physical therapy, too."

Chasen didn't look too happy about that, but nodded and thanked the man.

"There's no way in hell I'm shutting it down for another two months," Noah said as the medic headed for the door. "I laid around on my ass for eight weeks already. I can't do that again. I'll go crazy!"

His boss scowled. "You and I both know you didn't rest that leg as much as you should have while you were on limited duty. I saw you running, biking, and lifting weights. I took you at your word that you were good to go and you obviously weren't."

Noah opened his mouth to say he was fine until that jackass fell on him, but Chasen cut him off.

"I'll call HQ when we get to the hotel and tell them you're going medical leave for sixty days. So, for the next two months, you're going to sit on your couch and play video games."

Noah ground his jaw. There was no way he could do nothing but sit around on his butt for that long.

Chasen must have expected him to argue because he held up his hand. "It's either that or you spend the next sixty days pushing paperwork."

Noah sighed. While the idea of sitting around doing nothing for two months scared the hell out of him, it was nothing compared to how terrified he was of becoming a desk jockey. If hanging out on his couch playing video games was what he had to do to get back on active duty, he'd handcuff himself to his frigging Xbox.

CHAPTER

San Diego, California

MAYBE IT WAS JUST A RANDOM BREAK-IN." PEYTON Matthews eyed the recently repaired sliding glass door and the section of living room floor that had been covered with broken glass until a little while ago. "That happens, you know."

While that might sound completely logical, one look at her best friend, Laurissa Bradley, and literary agent, Em Fuller, told Peyton that was probably wishful thinking. Both of them sat on the cushy sectional couch looking like they weren't buying it. Peyton had expected as much from Laurissa, since her friend had been with her when they'd gotten back from the movie theater last night and discovered someone had smashed in the back door. Laurissa had been freaking out ever since.

But Em, her no-nonsense agent with her bob hairdo and oversized eyeglasses, was supposed to be the calm, reasonable one. The clear-headed person in her corner who always advised Peyton to think through every situation and never jump to conclusions. She thought for sure Em would be the first one to tell her to relax and chill out. Instead, her agent had jumped on the first flight out of San Francisco the moment Peyton told her that someone had broken into her house. Em had landed in San Diego earlier that morning.

"Right," Em said, sharing a look with Laurissa. "Someone went to all the trouble to break in and the only things they took were your desktop computer and laptop? They left behind the TV, didn't ransack your closets and drawers looking for valuables or touch your jewelry armoire? I don't think so. They wanted your book, and we all know it."

Peyton flopped down on the other end of the sectional and blew out a breath. She'd been hoping against hope there was another answer here, but she knew Em was right. Someone had been trying to steal her manuscript, plain and simple.

"Is it really any surprise?" Laurissa asked, blue eyes knowing. "Your book releases in a few days and people are going crazy to get their hands on it. Whoever broke in probably thought they could get an advance copy if they grabbed your computers."

Peyton considered that. The next book in her young adult series was coming out soon and the anticipation had been building for so long that it was at a fever pitch, so she supposed Laurissa could be right.

"That makes sense, I guess. Not only would they have gotten a copy of the new book, but the next one in the series after that." She let out a snort. "I can just imagine the look on their face if they got their hands on both of them. It'd be like Christmas and their birthday rolled into one."

She might have said that last part in jest, but truthfully, she knew that most readers didn't realize how the writing process worked. She'd talked to hundreds of fans who assumed she finished writing a book, and then poof, a few days later, it was in bookstores. They had no idea she'd written this newest book last year. Or that the one she was furiously trying to get to her publisher in less than two weeks wouldn't be released until next year.

"Regardless of whether they knew what book they were trying to steal, I'm just glad you agreed to follow the extra security precautions your publisher insisted on or we'd all be screwed right now," Em said.

Peyton groaned at the reminder. At the time, she thought her publisher's demand that she write on a desktop computer with no internet connection instead of a laptop like she always did was the stupidest thing ever. And if that weren't enough, they'd wanted her to save the manuscript and all her notes on an external hard drive only. Talk about adding more to her workload. While it'd seemed ridiculous, she was glad they'd been so damn paranoid.

She opened her mouth to say as much, only to have a yawn steal the words right out of her mouth. Picking up her mug, she got to her feet. "I need more caffeine. Anyone else want more coffee?"

"I'll have some," Em said, holding out her cup.

Peyton glanced at Laurissa, but her friend shook her head.

Mugs in hand, Peyton walked around the big, granite island that separated the living room from the kitchen to get refills. This side of the house faced the ocean and as she poured the coffee, she gazed at the rough waves lapping against the sand on the beach below the house. Usually, the sight was calming, but after last night, she had a hard time focusing on the beauty.

As bad as it had been to come home to all the glass and the broken door, the night hadn't ended there. After calling 911, she and Laurissa had to wait for what seemed like forever at a neighbor's house for the police to show up. When they finally did, they checked the house to make sure no one was inside, then spent hours asking her questions as the rest of the cops looked for clues. She'd assumed crime scene techs would dust for prints or something, but they hadn't. A detective named Dwayne Harrison had come by, though. A nice guy with a friendly demeanor, he told her that he'd do his best to find whoever had broken in and stolen her stuff.

"Unfortunately, we see a couple hundred thousand computers stolen in the greater San Diego area every year," he added. "All the thief has to do is scrape the serial number stickers off and dump them at one of a thousand different pawn shops. The chances of us finding them is almost nil."

Em had arrived a little while after Detective Harrison left and they'd all spent the remaining hours of darkness getting the sliding glass fixed—thankfully, Laurissa had a friend who installed them, otherwise there'd be plywood covering the opening right now—and the place cleaned up before making a run to Best Buy so Peyton could buy a new laptop. Because, regardless of the break-in, she still had a book to turn in.

She added cream and sweetener to her coffee—nothing for Em—then carried both mugs into the living room.

"While I know readers can sometimes get a little obsessive about their favorite stories, it's still hard to believe that someone would go so far as to break into my house so they could get an early peek at the book." She set Em's mug on the coffee table in front of her before sitting down. "I mean, they're willing to risk jail time to read a book a few days early? That's insane."

"You're assuming it was a reader," Em said as she picked up her mug and took a sip, obviously not caring that the coffee was practically hot enough to burn off her tongue.

"What do you mean?" Laurissa asked. "It had to be a fanatical reader, right? Who else would want her book enough to break down her door to get it?"

"It's a lot more likely that the person who

broke in was a book pirate, or at least hired by one." Em placed her mug on the table, then sat back on the couch with a tired sigh. "Those jackasses have made a living stealing books within days of them hitting the market. It only makes sense that one of them would decide to change the paradigm and try to get your book early. It would give them days to make money with absolutely no competition. And imagine if they'd gotten book five and offered it up a few weeks after book four released? Readers who would normally never dream of buying from a piracy site would click the buy link without a second thought. Whoever could get their hands on an advance copy of one of your books would make millions. Tens of millions even."

"Wow," Laurissa murmured, looking more than a little surprised. "I never realized. I mean, sure, I know books get pirated—especially now that so many people read digital versions only—but I never thought about how they got them. That someone would break into a house and steal. Can't anything be done to stop them?"

Em shook her head. "Not much. If the person who broke in had actually gotten the book, they would have uploaded to some website within minutes and then it would be over. Almost all of the piracy sites are overseas in places that either don't have copyright laws or don't enforce them. Even when publishers are able to get one of the places put out of business, there's another to take its place. They're like zombies."

"Crap," Peyton breathed. "I hadn't even thought this could have been some piracy scheme gone bad. Do you really think that's what happened?"

"Probably." Em shrugged. "But truthfully, it doesn't really matter what I think. While you and Laurissa were out getting your new laptop, I talked to your publisher. They're worried this person was after your manuscript and that they might come after it again once they realize it's not on either of the computers they stole. That's why they want me to hire a bodyguard for you. The live-in, 24/7 kind of security."

Peyton blinked at her agent over the rim of her mug, glancing back and forth between Em and Laurissa, waiting for the punchline. "A live-in bodyguard? You're kidding, right?"

"No, I'm not kidding," Em said. "In fact, I have to say that I agree with them. If this really was an attempt to grab your book for pirating purposes, they'll almost certainly try again. No doubt about it."

"Oh, come on." Peyton set her mug down on the table with a thud. "I already keep the book on an external hard drive I take with me everywhere I go. And I promise I'll lock it in the safe at night. Isn't that enough?"

"No, it isn't." Em sighed. "Look, I'm not to trying scare you or anything, but you need to realize you could be in danger. At some point, if these people can't get your book the easy way, they might come after you to get it the hard way. And with that release party you have for book four coming up, it would be crazy to take the risk of going out in public without someone to protect you."

"Maybe she's right, Peyton," Laurissa said with a worried look on her face. "What if this person decides to break in here in the middle of the night while you're sleeping? With the kind of money you two are talking about, this person could decide to really hurt you."

Peyton considered that, hating to admit even to herself that she actually was getting a little scared now. "Even if you're right—and I'm not saying you are—how would this even work? I have a book due in two weeks and you know how I get around deadline time. I can't have some stranger living in my house watching me write. I'd never get anything done. And how could we possibly find someone capable and trustworthy at such short notice? What if you end up hiring someone who sells me out for a few thousand dollars if this damn book pirate offers them money?"

A part of Peyton knew that last part was far-fetched, but she hated the entire idea of a body-guard with a passion. She was a private person by nature. It sorta came with being a writer. It was nothing for her to go days—sometimes even weeks—without interacting with anyone in person. Well, except for Laurissa. The idea of having a stranger in her house made her more than a little uncomfortable.

Em was talking about the various personal security companies that were available, saying they could have several candidates brought in so Peyton could find someone she gelled with. Peyton didn't say anything, but she wasn't sure if that would help.

"There is another option," Laurissa said, her voice softer than normal for her petite but normally outgoing friend. "I know someone who's extremely well-trained. World class protection, actually. He could protect you and it wouldn't be weird since it wouldn't be a total stranger."

While Peyton frowned in confusion, wondering who Laurissa was talking about, Em looked intrigued. "You know someone with experience at protecting people who'd take on a new client at the drop of a hat like this?"

Laurissa smiled and nodded. "My brother, Noah. He's a Navy SEAL on the Team at Coronado, so it goes without saying that there would be nobody better in the world at keeping Peyton safe. He's on medical leave right now and going stir crazy in his apartment playing video games all day. He'd jump at any excuse to get out of his place for a while. And once I tell him it's for a friend, he'd probably do it for free."

Realizing her mouth was hanging open, Peyton quickly snapped it shut. She was having a big problem wrapping her head around the idea of a Navy SEAL—as in the kind of Navy SEAL who'd taken down Bin Laden—protecting her and her book. The entire concept was insane.

"If your brother is on medical leave, how can he keep an eye on Peyton?" Em asked. "We need someone healthy and capable."

Laurissa waved her hand dismissively. "He just twisted his knee playing volleyball and pulled some ligaments or something. The SEALs put him on medical leave because he can't do the stuff they want him to do right now—jump out of planes, swim the English Channel, ride a shark while chasing a nuclear submarine. You know, SEAL stuff. He's still more fit than 99 percent of the men on the planet and won't even break a sweat keeping Peyton safe."

Em thought about that for a moment before nodding, her expression telling Peyton she was already on board with Laurissa's crazy idea. Peyton, on the other hand, still wasn't so sure. While she'd seen loads of pictures of Laurissa's brother, and had heard so many stories about him she felt like he was a friend, the truth was that they'd never actually met. Wouldn't it still be weird to have him in her house 24/7 for the foreseeable future?

It was Laurissa's impossible-to-ignore doe eyes that finally swayed Peyton to agree with this ridiculous scheme. Laurissa was her best friend in the world and Peyton could never deny her anything. Besides, if the pictures she'd been seeing of Noah all these years was any indication, the man would be easy enough on the eyes to make her overlook the inconvenience of having him staying with her.

"Okay, I'll agree to let Noah be my bodyguard," she said, really hoping she didn't come to regret this decision. "But I insist that he gets paid. If my publisher is so hot and heavy about this, they can damn well foot the bill for it."

"Excellent!" Jumping to her feet, Laurissa did a little happy dance. "Now, I just have to call Noah and convince him to do it."

Peyton did a double take. "Wait a minute. I thought you said he'd jump at the chance to do this. Now you're saying he might not?"

Laurissa simply waved her hand again as she reached for the cell phone in her back pocket. "Noah can be stubborn sometimes, but he can't say no to me. I'm his Kryptonite."

Noah took in the beach front property as he walked up to the front door of the house Laurissa had given him the address for. A gorgeous two-story deal with lots of windows, it was the kind of place he'd never be able to afford in a million years. A part of him wondered how much a place like this cost, even as the other part shouted at him to turn around and get back in his SUV before it was too late.

"Chasen would absolutely lose his mind if he knew I was doing this," he muttered.

Noah shook his head as he realized he'd actually said the words out loud. Ten days into his medical leave and he was already talking to himself. At this rate, he'd be looking at a psychological evaluation and discharge before he ever had to worry about getting chaptered out of the Navy over his bum knee.

That medic over in Yemen had been right. Noah's ligaments were intact, but the military doctor he'd seen stateside had told him he was damn lucky. One more tweak of his knee before it fully healed and his career in the SEALs was toast. He needed to stay off it as much as possible, alternate ice and heat multiple times throughout the day and night and do the gentle range-of-motion exercises the physical therapist had shown him. If he did that for the next six weeks, he had a good shot at making it back to active duty.

And he'd intended to do just that. He really had. But barely ten days into his rehab, he was ready to say the hell with it all and run screaming into the mountains surrounding San Diego. He'd always known he wasn't the type to sit still for very long, but being told he had to essentially sit on his couch and do nothing for months was driving him insane.

So, when Laurissa called and asked for help protecting a friend, he hadn't even slowed down to consider it. He'd agreed before his sister had done more than told him the address.

Now that he was here, he was definitely having second thoughts. Well, first thoughts technically, since he sure as hell hadn't been thinking when he'd packed a bag and run over here like a brainless moron. He was a SEAL, not a bodyguard. What did he know about providing personal protection? He couldn't even carry a weapon in the States—at least not legally.

Not that it kept him from ringing the doorbell. That would be too smart. Instead, he nudged the little black button, listening as the soft chimes echoed through the big house on the other side of the door. When it opened a few seconds later, he was immediately attacked by the blond, half-pint bundle of energy known as his sister. Laurissa practically knocked him off his feet as she threw her arms around him. On the bright side, his bad knee didn't twinge at all from the impact. He considered that a major plus these days.

"You really came!" Laurissa said, still squeezing the stuffing out of him. "I know you said you would, but I was worried you'd change your mind and back out at the last moment."

"The thought never entered my mind," Noah said, only feeling a little bad he'd been considering exactly that right before ringing the doorbell. "All you ever have to do is call and I'll come running."

"Well, thanks again, big bro." She stepped back to look up at him with that smile of hers. "I didn't get a chance to tell you much over the phone, but my friend, Peyton, is an author. Someone broke into her house last night and we're pretty sure they were after the manuscript she's working on. We're worried they might come back and try again."

Noah slipped his sunglasses off as he stepped into the house. The idea someone broke in to steal a half-finished book sounded a little unlikely to him, but he didn't say anything. If it got him out of his boring ass apartment for a while, he'd go along with the gig.

"Peyton, meet Noah, Navy SEAL and my favorite brother," Laurissa said, giving him another grin as they walked into the living room. "Noah, this is Peyton Matthews, my best friend and greatest writer in the world. I know I've mentioned her to you before, but since you never listen to anything I say, I doubt you remember."

Noah didn't comment on that last part, since it was kind of true. He also didn't point out that he was her *only* brother. Instead, he focused his attention on his sister's friend, almost stumbling on the plush carpet when he got a good look at her. Peyton Matthews wasn't what he expected at all.

When Laurissa told him her friend was an author, he'd pictured an older woman who wore glasses and had gray hair. Like Angela Lansbury in those reruns of *Murder She Wrote* that his mother loved to watch. Not that he was downing on the main character, Jessica Fletcher, but clearly, his imagination had failed him in this case. Tall and slender with sexy curves and long, blond hair, the bluest eyes he'd ever seen, and possibly the most kissable lips in the world, Peyton Matthews was the most beautiful woman he'd ever seen.

Forcing himself to ignore how good the woman looked in the tank top and the long, flowing skirt she wore, Noah stepped forward, extending his hand.

"Nice to meet you, Ms. Matthews," he said, hoping he came off as professional and knowing he was probably failing miserably at it. "Laurissa said someone broke in last night and that you're worried they might come back?"

"If we're right about who this person was," a woman said from the direction of the kitchen and Noah turned to see a middle-aged woman with short, dark hair walking into the living room. "Then it's only a matter of time before they make another move. I'm Em Fuller, by the way," she added, holding out her hand. "Peyton's agent."

"And if you're wrong about the motives behind the break-in?" he asked, after the woman explained the whole piracy angle and how the book would have been long gone if not for it being stored on a hard drive Peyton carried with her everywhere she went.

If he heard something like this a month ago, Noah would have thought they were all being paranoid, but after the Yemen mission, he was starting to see these kinds of situations in a completely different light. That said, it was still more likely the break-in was nothing more than the random smash and-grab that it seemed like.

Em shrugged in answer to his question. "If

we're wrong, you get to spend a couple weeks relaxing while Peyton finishes writing this book and does a few promotional events like the book signing this coming Saturday. And in return, you get a nice paycheck at very little risk on your part."

Noah would be lying if he said he hadn't been hoping for at least a little action simply so he'd have something to do, but he immediately squashed that thought, not comfortable with the idea of Peyton being in danger for even a second. And any time spent with a woman as gorgeous as she was would definitely be well spent, even if all he did was sit on the couch and watch ESPN while she wrote her book.

"About the money," he began, but Em waved her hand.

"Peyton's publisher will pay your asking price."

"I wasn't worried about that," he said. "But as active-duty military, I'm not allowed to take on outside employment without my commander's approval. And since I'm supposed to be on medical leave, that isn't going to happen." He glanced at Peyton. "I'm hoping your publisher would be okay with donating whatever they were going to pay me to a military charity like the Wounded

Warrior Project or the Special Operations Warrior Foundation."

He could tell from Peyton's smile she thought that was an excellent idea. Em didn't have a problem with it, either.

They spent the next hour going over the details of what he'd be doing for the next couple weeks and what Peyton's schedule would be like, then Em was up and heading for the door.

"I think you have everything under control," she said, all of her attention focused on her cell phone. "If I hurry, I should be able to make an afternoon flight back to San Francisco and get home before midnight."

There were a scary number of hugs between the three women before Laurissa announced she was leaving, too.

"I'd love to stay and hang out, but I know you're probably freaking about being behind on your word count, so I'm going to leave you in my brother's capable hands and let you get some work done," she said to Peyton. "Promise you won't write too long today, okay? You didn't get any sleep last night and I know you're already running on fumes."

Peyton gave his sister another hug, promising

to get her rest and eat right. To say that she and Laurissa were best friends seemed like an understatement. They were like sisters.

The silence that filled the house after Laurissa and Em left verged on being uncomfortable. He got the feeling Peyton wasn't used to having guys staying at her place. For some reason, the notion made him happy.

"I guess I should show you around a little, huh? You probably need to know where my bedroom is at least," Peyton said casually, only to freeze when she realized exactly what she'd just said. He was pretty sure she actually blushed a little. Noah decided it was kind of adorable.

"I do need to have a look around," he said, acting like he hadn't noticed her embarrassment. "But if you don't mind, I'd like to check the exterior of the property first. Then you can show me around in here."

She nodded, giving him a smile that lit up the room. "Sounds good. I've been going on coffee and adrenaline since coming home and finding the back door smashed in last night, so I was going to make a sandwich. I can make a couple for you, too, if you want?"

"I never turn down a sandwich." He returned

her smile. "Then again, there are very few foods I will turn down, so that's not saying much. I'll only be outside ten or fifteen minutes, but don't feel like you have to wait to eat on my account."

"I don't mind waiting." Peyton flashed him another smile as she headed for the kitchen. "Besides, it'll probably take me that long to make lunch."

Noah laughed, pretty sure she was joking. If the gourmet kitchen was anything to go by, Peyton knew her way around in there.

Slipping on his sunglasses, he walked outside, stepping off the porch and onto the front lawn. As he made his way around the exterior of the house, he swept the perimeter of the property with his gaze, looking for hiding spots a person could use to recon the house, or routes someone might take if they were going to sneak up on the place.

He paid special attention to the grass as he walked, looking for places that had been trampled flat recently. More than likely, whoever had broken in had probably spent time casing the house first. Maybe he'd find a shoe impression, a discarded cigarette butt, or piece of bubblegum. Anything with DNA on it like that might help the police find the dirtbag. Yeah, the cops had probably done this already, but it didn't hurt to look again.

Unfortunately, after two complete circuits of the property, he hadn't found anything remotely resembling a DNA sample. Hell, he hadn't found anything to make him think anyone had ever stepped foot onto Peyton's property.

Noah blew out a breath, his gaze wandering to the beach about twenty feet below the bluff he was standing on, the rough waves slapping up against the shore. The sound of the ocean never failed to calm him, and it didn't let him down now. Did Peyton feel the same draw since she lived on the beach?

While her house was undeniable beautiful, and the view incredible, the whole place was also completely indefensible. A person could access the property from a hundred different directions. The beach front was simply the easiest.

He cursed in frustration. When he'd jumped at Laurissa's offer to do this gig, he hadn't thought of it as anything more than a way to get out of the apartment. But now that he'd met Peyton and seen how scary all of this was for her, the gravity of the situation was quickly becoming much more real.

While he hoped Peyton and her agent were wrong and that the break-in was merely some random thing, it would be dangerous to think that way. If there really was an idiot out there willing to risk a prison term to steal her book, it was almost a certainty the guy would be back. And this time, the asshole might come at Peyton directly instead of trying to swipe the book covertly. He might have taken the job because he was bored, but he wasn't going to risk a woman's life simply because he'd gotten into this whole thing for the wrong reasons.

Of course, there was also the fact that Noah was more than a little attracted to Peyton. It would be silly to say that as a professional he should be able to deny that, because he couldn't. Noah dated, but not regularly. Between training, deployments, and the stress of being a SEAL, he didn't have the time or inclination to do much more than that. He'd never gotten deeply involved with any of the women he'd been with, but at the same time, he'd always been open to the idea of getting serious. If he found the right woman.

Not that he was saying Peyton was that woman, of course. Hell, he'd just frigging met her. But she definitely intrigued him. The issue would be getting to know her while his focus was on keeping her safe.

Turning, Noah started back toward the house, only to stop when his phone rang. The moment he saw Chasen's name on the screen, he considered letting it go to voice mail, but it'd be just his luck that the chief would show up at his apartment looking for him and figure out Noah wasn't home like he was supposed to be.

Taking a deep breath, he thumbed the green button.

"What's up, Chasen?"

"Just checking in to see how you're doing. I haven't talked to you in a few days and wanted to see how the knee was feeling."

"It's good," Noah said, pleased to think he was actually being honest this time. "No pain or instability. Taking care of it like the doc ordered."

Chasen started to say something, but then stopped. "Did I just hear a seagull in the background? Are you outside?"

Dammit.

Noah considered his options, immediately tossing out the most obvious lies about the TV being on, his window being open, or his neighbor having a pet bird. Instead, he decided to blend BS with the truth and see how far that got him.

"Yeah, I'm out on the beach," he said casually. "The physical therapist thinks it's a good idea to go for short walks on the sand. The uneven footing is supposed to help my knee from getting stiff. I'm not sure how well its working, but it beats being stuck inside all day."

There was silence on the other end of the line for a really long time and Noah thought for sure that he'd been made, but Chasen only sighed. "Okay, good. I was worried for a second you were out doing something stupid."

If the chief only knew.

"No way. I'm playing it smart this time. I'm not going to do anything to mess up my rehab and jeopardize my career."

"Good to hear," Chasen said. "I'll let you get back to your walk then. Just don't push too hard."

"Definitely not," Noah assured him. "I've got some sandwiches with my name on them waiting for me inside, then it's back to doing a whole lot of nothing."

CHAPTER
Two

IF THERE WAS ONE THING PEYTON HATED MORE THAN BEING behind on her word count, it was missing her morning yoga workout. Thanks to that moron who broke in last night, she'd be lucky if she could slip in a few downward dog poses between chapters today.

But right now, she couldn't do either until she ate something. Sighing, she glanced down at the plate piled high with sandwiches and made a face. Maybe she'd gone a little overboard. *Then again,* she thought as she caught sight of Noah walking across the lawn toward the house, *he is a big, muscular guy.*

Thinking about the hotness that was Noah made her head spin a little. While she'd seen plenty of photos of Laurissa's older brother, meeting him in person had been an eye opener. She probably shouldn't be thinking this way about her best friend's brother, but damn, the man was completely droolworthy.

Peyton guessed he was a few years older than she was, making him somewhere in his mid to late twenties. Tall and broad shouldered, he had thick, dark hair, eyes the color of her favorite chocolate bar, and a chiseled jaw with the perfect amount of stubble. And from the way that dark blue T-shirt molded to his chest, it was impossible to miss how well he was built. If someone asked her to find a poster boy for male perfection, it would definitely be Noah Bradley.

Even his name was perfect. Like one she'd use for a hero in her books. Strong and silent, attractive and sexy, a little mysterious, and more than a little dangerous.

Peyton snapped out of her silly thoughts at the sound of footsteps behind her. She turned to see the aforementioned hunk walking into the kitchen, regarding her with those beautiful dark eyes of his. Her gaze drifted to his jean-clad legs, remembering what Laurissa had said about her brother injuring his knee. He wasn't limping that she could tell. In fact, she wouldn't have been able to pick out which leg was causing him trouble if her life depended on it.

Realizing she was staring, she self-consciously reached up to tuck her hair behind her ear. "Sandwiches are made, if you're ready to eat. I have water, coconut-almond milk, and iced tea."

"Iced tea is fine, thanks," he said.

Picking up the plate of sandwiches, he brought it over to the kitchen table while Peyton got the drinks.

"Sorry I don't have anything other than tuna sandwiches to offer, but the cabinets start getting a little bare as I get near a deadline for a book," Peyton said as she set the glasses on the table.

Noah was already standing beside the chair closest to the wall waiting for her, so she took the one opposite him. Something told her that a dangerous man like him always liked to sit with his back to the wall so he'd be able to scope out the rest of the room for inbound trouble.

She almost laughed at that. Man, she *really* needed to get a life outside the books she wrote.

"Tuna's fine. Remember what I said about not turning down food," he said, flashing her a grin as he reached for one of the sandwiches and transferred it to his plate. Damn, he had a nice smile. "I take it you don't leave the house too much as you get closer to crunch time?"

She nodded, helping herself to a sandwich. "It doesn't seem to matter how fast I write when

I start a book, I always have to rush to finish it. Going grocery shopping is the first thing to go in that situation."

"You could always order online and have it delivered, you know?" he pointed out.

"I could," she admitted. "And when I'm desperate, that's what I do. But at a certain point, I get so far behind that I don't even want to waste time filling out the order. And forget about putting the stuff away once it gets here."

He chuckled, taking a bite of his sandwich. "I can picture it now—bags of food sitting in the middle of the kitchen for days while you come in every once in a while to dig out a box of Pop Tarts."

She laughed. "That's about the way it works. Except it's not Pop Tarts, it's Honey Nut Cheerios. I think I'm addicted to the stuff."

He took another bite, chewing thoughtfully. "So, you haven't left the house in a while, except for last night. Who knew you were going out?"

The sudden nature of the question caught her off guard. One second they were laughing and talking about Pop Tarts and Cheerios, the next he'd gone all intense on her.

"Laurissa is the only one who knew. She showed up and dragged me out to see a movie and grab dinner. You don't suspect your own sister was involved in the break-in, do you?"

"Definitely not, but you have to admit it's convenient as hell that your house gets broken into the one night you decide to go out, right? It means the thief was either incredibly lucky you were out or he was watching the place for a while and made his move the moment you left."

The coincidence hadn't been lost on Peyton. She and Laurissa had talked about it while the cops had poked around. They'd come up with dozens of convoluted and outlandish theories. Peyton *was* a writer. But Noah had cut through all their wild speculation in seconds with his bleak—and rather creepy—assessment of the situation. The idea that someone had been outside her house day and night watching her every move made the hair on the back of her neck stand on end.

"Which one do you think it is?"

She wasn't sure which she'd rather have him confirm. The first meant she was lucky to be alive, the second meant she had a determined stalker.

"I have no idea," Noah said with a casual shrug before taking another bite of his sandwich. "If we're lucky and the guy never comes back, that means we have our answer."

Peyton sipped her iced tea. "You keep referring to the person who broke in as a *he*. Is that based on any kind of evidence, or simply plain old sexism?"

Noah snorted, reaching for another sandwich. "Good point. Consider me properly chastised. I'll endeavor to be more inclusive when I'm talking about the thief."

"Don't worry about it. I figured it was a guy, too," she said. "I was merely hoping you knew something the cops didn't tell me."

"I wish I did," he admitted.

As they ate, Noah asked her to walk him through the events of last night's break-in one more time. That wasn't too difficult since she'd already gone over it at least twenty times for the police and then Em.

"What's up with saving your book to an external hard drive?" Noah asked, licking some avocado mayonnaise off his thumb in a way she shouldn't have found intriguing, but did for some reason. "Hasn't your publisher ever heard of the Cloud?"

Peyton laughed. "I asked them the same question. Unfortunately, they're sort of old school that way. When the third book in the series took off and became an international bestseller, they got worried someone would hack the Cloud and find the book or that someone on the inside would pluck it off and sell it to the highest bidder. I'm lucky. If they had their way, I'd be locked in an underground bunker somewhere writing this thing on a manual typewriter. The hard drive was the compromise."

"International bestseller, huh? I guess I can understand the paranoia." A frown marred his otherwise perfect features. "How many people know you carry the drive around with you all the time?"

"Not many. Em and Laurissa, of course, and a few people at my publisher."

"That's good," Noah murmured. "If there really is someone determined to get their hands on your book and he discovers you carry it with you every time you go out, he's more likely to come after you instead of trying to break in to your house again."

She shuddered. "Then let's hope they never learn about the hard drive."

Noah picked up his glass, regarding her over the top of it. "Laurissa told me that you guys went to San Diego State together. Did you go to college for creative writing or something like that?"

"Not exactly," she said. "I've always loved books and reading since I was a kid. I wrote stuff all through middle and high school, but nothing serious. Just goofing around, you know? I went to SD State to get an undergraduate degree in English and my master's in education. I figured it would be a natural fit for me."

"And it wasn't?"

She laughed again. It was easy to do that with him, she realized, which was kind of crazy. It usually took her forever to get comfortable with a guy, but with Noah, it was like she didn't even have to try. "Actually, it was. I taught for a couple of years. Teaching is a ton of work for sure—don't ever let anyone tell you differently—but I enjoyed it."

"Okay, so how does one go from being a hard-working English teacher to an international best seller?"

"The normal way, I guess. By pure accident." She smiled as she thought about how many times she'd told this story at book signings and conferences. It was something *everyone* wanted to know. "During summer breaks I wrote stuff for one of the big fan fiction sites. It wasn't meant to be anything more than a fun way to relieve a little stress. But then Em sent me an email saying she liked my voice and wanted to know if I had any original material. I sent her what I had and about a year later, the first book in my young adult series hit the stands. It kind of exploded from there."

He seemed to consider that for a moment before answering. "I'm probably going to shock you by admitting I actually *do* know what fan fiction is, but even then, it sounds like an amazing ride."

She laughed, imagining the big Navy SEAL leaning over his iPhone reading *Harry Potter* fan fic. "Amazing is a good word for it. One minute, I'm barely covering the rent on my apartment, and the next, I'm resigning from my teaching position so I can write full time. I might have loved teaching, but I couldn't pass up the chance to chase a dream."

"Did you grow up in the San Diego area?" he asked, changing direction with his question. "Since you went to State, I'm assuming you did."

"Nope. I grew up in San Francisco." She shrugged. "And while I love it there, there was no way I could pass up a chance to go to someplace warm enough where you can actually swim in the water. And once I got used to the weather, there was no way I was moving back."

Noah let out another chuckle. "I get that. I

went swimming in the San Francisco Bay once during a training exercise and definitely didn't enjoy it."

They talked for a bit longer about what it was like growing up in warm, sunny San Diego versus the frequently sunny, but not-so-warm San Francisco. Before long, Noah had polished off the rest of the sandwiches, and she realized she'd spent a lot longer on lunch than she'd planned.

She glanced at her watch. "Crap. I need to write."

"Yeah, of course," he said. "I'm sorry. I didn't mean to keep you from your book. If you could give me a quick tour of the house first...?"

Peyton opened her mouth to tell him it wasn't like that and that she didn't mind spending time with him, but then remembered Noah was there to protect her, not hang out with her. He wanted to get on with his job.

"Sure," she said, quickly getting to her feet and feeling a little silly she'd been gabbing away with the guy hired to be her bodyguard. Like he didn't have anything better to do. "You've already seen most of the downstairs, so it won't take long."

As Peyton headed for the stairs, she was

extremely aware of Noah walking behind her, and she suddenly found herself wondering if he was checking out her butt. Reminding herself that they weren't in one of her books, she hurried up the rest of the steps, quickly pointing out the guest room, workout room, the home office where she did her writing, and a spare bathroom.

"My bedroom is the one at the end of the hall," she added.

"Does your boyfriend stay over often?" he asked, his dark gaze surveying her bedroom, eyes lingering for a moment on the king-sized bed with its soft blue paisley-print blanket before turning to look toward the en suite bathroom beyond.

Thank goodness Noah wasn't looking her way or he would have seen her standing there gaping like a carp.

"What?" she finally managed to squeak, hoping it would give her a little more time to gather her thoughts.

"Your boyfriend?" He swung his gaze back to her. "I assume he spends the night occasionally and need to know when so I can make myself scarce."

Blushing, she slowly shook her head. In truth, her dating life was nonexistent. But it wasn't her fault. She'd gone out with guys in college and had been in a relationship for a while after graduating, but nothing had come of it. Dating had taken a backseat once her writing career took off. Hell, she hadn't even been out with a guy since sometime during the middle of book two in her series. Or had it been the beginning of book three? It was hard to remember. She liked to blame her lack of social life on her writing schedule, but honestly, she hadn't met anyone who sparked enough of an interest to bother. But maybe that was changing.

"You don't have to worry about that," she said. "I'm sort of between boyfriends at the moment, so no guys will be hanging around."

"Except me," he murmured.

Peyton was sure she saw a flicker of something in his chocolate-brown eyes, though before she could be sure, he stepped past her into the hallway.

"Yup, just you," she said, only realizing how sad that sounded once it was out.

When he didn't respond, she decided he probably hadn't heard her anyway, which was fortunate.

"So, this bodyguard thing," she said, catching up with him in the hallway. "How does it work?

Do you follow me around all the time, or will you be somewhere in hiding, ready to come running when I scream for help?"

He gave her a smile. "Less of the first and more of the second."

She refused to touch the innuendo with a ten-foot pole. "So, I simply go about my business like normal, writing and stuff?"

"Yup. You do whatever you usually do, go wherever you usually go, and I'll stay in the background. You won't even know I'm here."

Um, right.

Peyton seriously doubted she'd forget a man like Noah was hanging out in her house. He was sort of hard to miss, even when he wasn't in the same room.

She cleared her throat, motioning toward her home office. "Okay then. I'm going to hang out up here and get some writing done. Feel free to grab something else to eat or drink if you want. I'll be up here...just writing."

Noah smiled again, then turned and headed downstairs. Peyton watched him disappear down the steps. How the hell was she ever going to get any writing done when her hunky bodyguard had taken up residence in her head?

CHAPTER
Three

NOAH MADE ANOTHER CIRCUIT AROUND THE OUTSIDE of the house after going downstairs, then stood on the bluff gazing at the water again. It was crazy when he realized how long it had been since he'd gone for a swim in the ocean. Even before the mission in Yemen, he'd laid off the deep-sea workouts, trying to baby his knee. It had been nearly five weeks since he even tried it. Watching the deep blue water rise and fall, and seeing the waves lap onto the sand made him eager to do it again. But that would have to wait until after this bodyguard gig. Besides, his knee was doing good. He didn't want to do anything to screw it up.

He headed over to the front of the house to grab his overnight bag from his SUV. His mouth curved as he thought of Peyton, replaying the stuff they'd talked about at lunch, then while she'd been showing him around the place. The mere suggestion that a woman as attractive, intelligent, and witty as Peyton could be in between boyfriends seemed too insane to consider. How could there not be a line of men a mile long trying to get with her?

He was still thinking about that as he rounded the corner of the house and saw a Black F-150 truck pulling up next to his SUV. He barely had a chance to recognize the vehicle before Sam, Wes, and Lane jumped out and headed for the front door, all three dressed in camouflage uniforms. What the hell were they doing here in the middle of a work day?

Knowing there was only one way to answer that question, he hurried to intercept them before they could ring the doorbell.

"I assume you guys are looking for me," he said as they all turned his way. "Though to be honest, I'm more interested in how you found me than in why."

Sam grinned. "Chasen mentioned you were out walking on the beach, so we knew something was up considering how much you frigging hate exercising on sand. When we stopped by your place, a neighbor said you left hours ago with an overnight bag, so I called your sister. She ratted you out in nothing flat."

Noah ground his jaw. There were definitely disadvantages to having friends who knew him so well. Not only did Sam know Laurissa's number, but also how much he hated exercising on the beach. Ever since going through the twenty-four weeks of hell that was Basic Underwater Demolition/SEAL training, where running through the surf and sand until you puked was a near daily occurrence, he had a thing about working out there. He might love swimming in the ocean, but running—or even walking—on the sand? No way. Not unless someone forced him to do it.

"So, what's up?" Wes asked. "Laurissa wouldn't give us any details, only that you were at this address doing something important. What the hell, dude? You go out and get another job while on medical leave?"

He didn't say anything, because honestly, what the hell could he say that would explain any of this?

"Holy crap!" Lane said, looking at Noah in shock. "That's exactly what happened, isn't it? You got bored sitting around your apartment playing video games and decided to get a job."

Noah couldn't help but stare at the effing new guy. "What would you know? You've only been in the platoon for a month and we haven't spent more than fifteen minutes in the same room together."

Lane snorted. "Am I wrong?"

"No." Noah grimaced. "I never knew I was so transparent."

"Well, you are," Wes said. "But if you needed something to keep you occupied for a few hours a day, you could have volunteered to be a door greeter at Walmart or something. Not whatever this is." He gestured toward Peyton's house and the pricey piece of beach front property she owned. "You didn't get yourself mixed up in anything illegal, did you?"

Noah did a double take. "What? No! Why would you even think something like that?"

Wes shrugged. "You have to admit, our team has a history of making bad choices when it comes to the law. Hell, a couple months ago I spent the night in jail for one of my less stellar decisions. So, I'm in no position to judge if you decided to do something stupid."

Noah remembered. That situation had definitely been messy.

"Well, you can chill out," he said. "I don't claim to be brilliant, but I'm not reckless enough to get involved in anything illegal. The woman who lives here—Peyton Matthews—is a writer who's a friend of Laurissa's. Someone broke in last night while she was out and tried to steal the book she's writing. Her publisher wanted to hire a bodyguard and Laurissa recommended me."

His Teammates stared at him like pigs looking at a Rolex.

"Very funny," Sam muttered. "What are you really doing here?"

Noah scowled. He supposed he couldn't blame the guys for not believing him. Noah barely believed it and he was living it.

"You're serious, aren't you?" Wes said when he didn't answer. "This house really belongs to Peyton Matthews, the writer? Hell, I don't even read romance and I've heard of her. And you're actually her bodyguard?"

"Yes, I'm serious," he said. "Yes, this is really Peyton Matthew's house. And yes, I'm actually her bodyguard. But if it makes you feel any better, I'm not taking any payment for it. I asked the publisher to donate the money to a military charity."

Noah filled them in on the whole story, including the part about Peyton storing her book on a hard drive she carried around with her, and the working theory that whoever was trying to get their hands on the book might be connected to some kind of book pirating operation.

"If you need backup, just ask," Sam said. "If we aren't on alert status for another treasury mission, we'll be here."

Knowing his buddies had his back meant a lot to him and Noah was about to thank him for the offer when his head caught up to the other stuff Sam said.

"Thanks. I'll definitely call if I need any help, but what do you mean about another treasury mission?" He was curious even if he couldn't be a part of it. "I thought we were officially done with that after we left Yemen."

"Apparently not," Sam said. "Agent Woods has been given the unenviable task of tracking down and capturing Magpie. They've moved him to the San Diego field office so he can be close enough to reach out if he decides he needs tactical support. We deploy the second we get confirmation they've found Magpie."

"But the Treasury Department has to know there's almost no way they're ever going to find Magpie," Noah said. "They never had a clue who he was to begin with and now that he knows someone is after him, they never will."

"Agreed, but Woods drags us into daily intelligence briefings to go over possible sightings anyway," Wes said. "There's no other word to describe it except painful, but Chasen wants us on alert for whenever Woods calls. Speaking of which, we better get back before the chief gets suspicious."

Noah nodded. He definitely didn't want Chasen finding out he was doing this bodyguard gig, especially since he'd already lied to him about it. The chief always took care of his Team, but it still wouldn't end well for Noah.

"Hey, before we go," Lane said, "do you think you could introduce us to Peyton Matthews? I mean, since we're here and all. I'm sort of a fan of hers."

Noah stared, stunned Lane read the kind of books Peyton wrote.

"Maybe some other time," he finally said. "Peyton has a book due soon and is trying to finish it on time."

"Okay, that's cool. I get it." Lane's shoulders sagged for a minute before he grinned. "Hey, why don't you can bring her to the party Friday night? She can't write all the time."

Noah frowned in confusion. "What party?"

"It's a platoon promotion party," Sam answered, giving him a grin. "Nash got promoted to Petty Officer 1st Class and I made Petty Officer 2nd Class. We're pooling our money and having one big party. You should definitely bring Peyton. Hell, invite Laurissa, too. We're going to find a restaurant with a private room, so we can let loose."

Noah doubted Peyton would want to go hang out with people she didn't know, especially when she had a book due. Inviting Laurissa along might help, though. And he definitely wouldn't mind spending some time with the Team. He was barely two weeks into his medical leave and he already missed the camaraderie.

"I'll ask her," he said with a shrug. "Laurissa, too."

His buddies left a little while after that, but not before Sam got another promise from Noah that he'd call if he needed help.

Grabbing his bag, he headed for the front door. Thinking he should let her know he was back inside, he set his bag on the floor beside the sectional couch and headed upstairs to her office. He heard the clicking of the keyboard before he even reached the top of the stairs. Damn. If the sound was any indication, she typed fast. Like a cheetah-on-caffeine fast.

He poked his head in the open doorway to see her sitting at her desk, her back turned three-quarter to him, iPhone AirPods shoved in her ears, head moving rhythmically to whatever tunes she was listening to, fingers moving in a blur across the keyboard of the laptop. If he wasn't seeing actual words appear on the screen, he would have thought she was typing gobbledygook.

Noah was about to walk away, not wanting to disturb Peyton when she was obviously on a roll, but then she started singing softly in time with her head bobs...something about X's and O's. The sound was so breathy yet adorable, it was impossible not to watch.

He must have stood there a good five minutes, entranced at the sight of Peyton typing away on her book, singing along with her music, pausing every once in a while to lift her hands up and dance around in her seat.

Damn, it was adorable.

Back downstairs, Noah considered turning on ESPN, but worried the noise might bother Peyton, even if she was listening to music. Then the bookshelf along the wall caught his eye. He walked over to graze a little, immediately becoming intrigued when he realized one of the shelves was full of book Peyton had written. Thinking about what Lane had said about reading them, he pulled one out deciding to give it a look.

The cover was a smaller version of one of the posters upstairs in her office, featuring a good-looking guy with a pretty girl. Admittedly, it wasn't his usual reading, but curiosity made him flip through it. It only took him a second to find the first book in the series, and when he had it, Noah moved over to the couch and sat down. If nothing else, maybe it'd keep him occupied for a bit.

Before he knew it, he found himself lost in the story. It might have started simply as a distraction, but Noah soon admitted it was good. Damn good. Having enlisted in the Navy right out of high school, he never went to college like the characters in Peyton's books, but he could relate to them anyway. Maybe because when you got right down to it, a lot of the crap the characters went through wasn't so different than what he'd dealt with as a young SEAL. Figuring out who you wanted to be, the kinds of people you wanted to associate with, the path you would take in the world, where you even wanted to go with your life. He guessed those were universal issues, no matter where you were in the world and what you were doing.

Then again, it could also be because he had a younger sister who'd spent a lot of time talking his ear off about her time in college, friends, boys, course loads, and the various life crises she went through.

Noah finished the first book and was heading for the second when he realized it was almost 1730—five-thirty. He'd been reading for quite a while. He thought about asking Peyton if she was hungry, but when he sauntered over to the bottom of the stairs he heard the sound of rapidly clicking keys. He didn't want to interrupt her when she was on a roll.

He ended up ordering some pizza, grabbing a couple slices for himself and putting the rest in the fridge, then lost himself in Peyton's second book. He was done with those slices and devouring a few more, halfway through the book, before she came downstairs. It was dark outside, and a quick glance at his watch told him it was after eight already. He wasn't sure how she could write for that long, but judging by the number of books on the shelf, she definitely could.

"There's more pizza in the fridge," he said, glancing up as she headed into the kitchen.

She came out a few moments later with a slice of microwaved cheese and pepperoni in one hand and a glass of iced tea in the other.

"Hope you don't mind that I grabbed one of your books to read," he said as she sat down on the other side of the sectional.

"Not at all." Her lips curved into a smile. "I didn't peg you for a romance reader, though."

He chuckled. "I never thought I was. But yours are good. Not too much of the mushy stuff."

"Thank you...I think." Laughing, Peyton took a bite of her pizza, holding the plate under her like she was afraid she might make a mess. "Mmm, this is delicious."

"Can't go wrong with pizza," he said. "In fact, I damn near live on the stuff. I could eat it every night of the week."

"Better not tell your significant other that." She eyed him, pizza poised in hand for another bite. "She'd probably want you to slip in something different now and then, like fruits and veggies."

Noah wasn't sure how they'd gone from talking about pizza to his relationship status. But he knew when a woman was fishing for personal info and why she might be doing it. Hell, he'd done it himself a few hours ago. He'd be lying if he said he wasn't stoked knowing Peyton was interested in him that way.

"I'm sure she would if there was a significant other," he said. "But there isn't, so I get to eat pizza any time I want."

Peyton's expression didn't change, but Noah thought he detected the slightest trace of satisfaction there now. But it disappeared as she went back to eating and he had to question if maybe she was a much better player than he'd assumed. That only made him more intrigued than he'd already been.

"I have a bunch of other take-out menus in the top drawer to the left of the oven." She gave him a smile. "If you decide you need to break up the pizza routine, I mean."

"I'll keep that in mind." He set down the book to pick up his plate and the half-eaten slice still on it. "How'd the writing go? It certainly seemed like you were in the groove if the clicking of the keys is any indication."

"Actually, it went much better than I thought it would." She sipped her iced tea. "With everything that happened last night, I was worried I wouldn't be able to focus, but I got on a roll and knocked out about five thousand words."

He shook his head. "Damn, that sounds like a lot. Does that mean you're done for the night?"

Peyton yawned, then let out another laugh. "Oh, I'm definitely done. I'm going to eat another slice of pizza, take a quick shower, then try to catch up on all the sleep I missed last night."

Noah had an image of a naked Peyton standing underneath a spray of warm water with soap suds running down her body. The thought was enough to make him want to groan, but fortunately she chose that moment to stand and head into the kitchen for that next slice of pizza, giving him a few seconds of privacy to get his perverted thoughts back together.

"The bed in the guest room upstairs is already made up," Peyton said from the kitchen as she hit the button on the microwave. "Laurissa sleeps over all the time, so I keep it ready with clean sheets and stuff."

As much as he liked the idea of sleeping in a nice comfy bed a few feet away from Peyton, that wasn't a good idea. He was here to guard the woman, not lust over her.

"Actually, I'll be sleeping down here on the couch," he said.

She walked into the living room, a baffled look on her face. "Seriously?"

"Yeah. If anyone does tries to break in, they'll have to go through me before reaching the stairs and the second floor," he said. "That should give you enough time to get out of bed, grab your phone, and bail out the window. I know it looks like a long drop, but the grass is soft, so you'll handle the fall okay. After that, run to the nearest neighbor and call the cops."

Peyton stared at him for a few long seconds, fear in her eyes. "Do you really think someone might try and break in during the middle of the night?"

"Do I think it will happen? Probably not," he said. "But I need to be ready in case it does. So, I'm sleeping down here, okay?"

She studied him for another moment before nodding. "Okay. There are sheets, blankets, and pillows in the linen closet at the top of the stairs and the bathroom down here has its own shower if you need it. Have a good night," she added as she headed upstairs, carrying her glass and the remainder of her pizza slice.

"You, too."

Noah's gaze locked on her spectacular butt as she disappeared up the steps. He knew he shouldn't be staring, but it was hard not to. He recalled the conversation he had with himself earlier when he wondered if he could have something with a woman he was supposed to be keeping safe. Still not having an answer to that question, he stood and headed for the kitchen, hoping another slice of pizza might help him figure out how he was going to get through this whole thing with his sanity intact.

CHAPTER

AFTER THE TERRIFYING IMAGE NOAH HAD LEFT HER WITH last night about someone breaking in and having to throw herself out a window to run screaming through the neighborhood, Peyton had been sure she'd never get to sleep. As it turned out, she'd slept like a rock. But as she lay snuggled in her blankets, she decided that's what you got when you had a big, strong, Navy SEAL sleeping downstairs protecting you with his life. It was impossible not to feel safe around him and all those muscles. And she had to admit that intensity as he'd told her exactly what she should do if anyone broken in was incredibly attractive. Yeah, that thing about dangerous men was a cliché but it worked for her.

Still foggy with sleep, Peyton rolled onto her back and stretched her arms over her head, smiling up at the ceiling. She probably could have been a little more subtle last night when it came to finding out if Noah was married or otherwise spoken for. But how else was she supposed to figure out if he was single or not? Besides, guys were usually oblivious to stuff like that, so she doubted he even noticed she was interested in him.

Not that she thought there was any chance of spending time with him after this whole bodyguard thing was done. He was attractive, easy to talk to, and fun to be around, but he was a Navy SEAL for heaven's sake. He probably had hundreds of women throwing themselves at him whenever he wanted female company. There was no reason for him to ever spend time with a bookworm like her.

Yet, despite all that, she still liked knowing Noah was officially single. It made her feel less guilty daydreaming about him. She didn't want to feel like a homewrecker, even in her fantasies. It was probably strange, but she'd decided long ago that being a little strange was okay.

She lay there a few minutes longer, listening for sounds of movement downstairs and wondering if Noah was awake yet. She didn't hear anything. Then again, he was a SEAL. Wasn't stealth his middle name?

Telling herself she'd find out soon enough, Peyton hopped out of bed and crossed the carpet into the bathroom to brush her teeth. Minty fresh, she put on some lip gloss and a light coating of mascara, then put her hair up in a loose twist and pulled on a tank top and a pair of yoga pants. While she felt good about the writing she'd finally gotten done yesterday, there was no way she was missing her yoga session this morning. She needed it to get herself mentally back on track.

She padded barefoot out of the bedroom, heading downstairs to get some water before starting her session. Her bell bottoms flapped softly around her ankles as she moved and she slowed her steps, not wanting to wake Noah if he was still sleeping. When she got to bottom, she froze. It was either that or stumble and fall flat on her face.

Noah stood by the couch, his back to her as he folded the sheets and a blanket he'd found in her linen closet. Not that she cared about his folding skills at the moment, not when he was standing there wearing nothing but a pair of tight-fitting boxer briefs. Suddenly, breathing was much more difficult than normal. She guessed this is what people meant when they used the term *breathtaking*.

Peyton had never really paid much attention to a guy's back before, but with those wide shoulders tapering to a trim waist, Noah's was truly beautiful. It was all she could do not to step over there and run her hands over all that sculpted muscle.

Then he turned around and her jaw dropped.

All Peyton could do was stare. He looked good from the back, but from the front... Well, *daaaaammn*, was all that came to mind. He was all chiseled chest, washboard abs, sleek biceps, and well-muscled legs. She'd never seen a guy so well-built in her life. Clearly, all the training SEALs did paid off. Her gaze wandered lower to the tight boxer briefs he wore. They left little to the imagination, and she stood there, eyes locked on the obvious bulge.

When she finally lifted her head, she found Noah regarding her with a sexy glint in his chocolate-brown eyes, clearly unselfconscious that he was standing there in his underwear. And that she was looking. Not that he had any reason to be embarrassed. He looked like a Greek god come to life. And truthfully, Peyton had no reason to be embarrassed, either. Noah was a man standing in the middle of her living room in his underwear.

She was a woman looking at someone she found attractive, one who obviously didn't mind her looking.

Peyton blushed anyway.

She wet her suddenly dry lips. "I...um...came down to grab a bottle of water. I'm going to do some yoga. I didn't mean to interrupt what you were doing. You're welcome to make coffee and grab something for breakfast if you want."

He tossed the folded blanket on the couch, then stacked the pillow neatly on top of it. "You didn't interrupt anything. I've been up for a while. I'll get right on that coffee, though. You want some before you start your workout?"

Peyton's eyes locked on his bare chest for one long moment before she mentally kicked herself for staring—again. Recovering, she shook her head. "No, thanks. Coffee and yoga don't really mix well."

Careful not to let her eyes wander anymore, she forced herself to walk into the kitchen. It might have been her imagination, but she thought she felt Noah's gaze follow her. She resisted the urge to look over her shoulder as she ducked into the fridge for a bottle of water. Unfortunately, the blast of frigid air did nothing to cool her down.

When she came out again, Noah had already put on his jeans and was reaching for his T-shirt.

Peyton didn't know whether to be disappointed or relieved.

Giving him a nod, she hurried upstairs and into her workout room. On the same side of the house as her bedroom, both spaces faced the beach, though this room had extra big windows. It was an ideal space to work out in. Besides the mat she used for yoga, there was also a spinning bike, portable ballet barre, some free weights, and a television mounted on the wall.

Setting her bottle of water on the table underneath the TV, she popped in the DVD, then grabbed her yoga block and stood in the center of the mat. Hands in prayer, she took a deep breath. With its tranquil music and poses designed for strength and balance, yoga was her favorite form of exercise. As far as she was concerned, it was the perfect way to start each day.

Unfortunately, with images of a half-naked Noah constantly popping into her head, Peyton had a hard time focusing on what she was doing. That was the thing with yoga. It wasn't something you could go through the motions with. You had to be present and in-the-moment, breathing through each movement. If not, you ended getting almost nothing out of it.

Knowing she needed to get Noah out of her system, Peyton gave herself permission to fantasize about her half-naked SEAL bodyguard for a few minutes. After thinking about what it would have been like to walk downstairs and join him on the couch last night—or even better, invite him up to her bed—she was able to clear her mind and get back to her workout. By the time she finished her regular thirty-minute session, she'd almost forgotten she even had a bodyguard.

She slipped from chaturanga smoothly into downward dog, really feeling the release in her lower back, when she sensed movement near the door. She glanced that way to see Noah standing there staring at her butt.

Pulse quickening, Peyton slowly lowered herself to her knees, then half-turned to look at him over her shoulder to see him eyeing her intently. She'd never had a man look at her that way, all heat and hunger. It made her feel warm all over, most of that feeling settling right between her thighs. As he continued to stand there without saying anything, she had to wonder how long he'd been watching her.

"Is something wrong?" she finally forced herself to ask, the words coming out a little less stable than she'd intended.

She watched as Noah gave himself a little shake, as if he'd just realized he was staring. "Oh. No. Everything's fine. Laurissa's here. She wanted to know if you had time to talk."

"I always have time for Laurissa." Peyton pushed herself upright and got to her feet. "But she already knows that. Why didn't she come upstairs herself?"

Noah shrugged. "Because my sister is a weirdo, maybe? She walked in the front door and straight into the kitchen to grab a cup of coffee, then headed out to the back deck saying she'd wait for you out there. Hope I didn't bother you by coming up."

"No, of course not," she assured him. "Feel free to come upstairs anytime you want."

As they walked, Peyton swore Noah let her get a little ahead of him so he could sneak another glimpse at her butt, and she felt her body go warm again as she realized she liked it.

Noah had to admit he'd never given yoga pants much thought until he'd seen Peyton in them. The stretchy material hugged her curvy butt, not to mention made her legs look a mile long. She was so sexy in them that he could barely remember his own name. Which was probably why he'd forgotten that he was standing there in Peyton's living room in nothing but his underwear. At least until he'd followed the direction of her gaze and noticed she was fixated on something south of his belt line.

It was an understatement to say Peyton was a beautiful woman. But wearing yoga pants—and blushing—she was damn near a goddess.

He'd barely managed to push the images of those sinfully sexy yoga pants out of his head when he went upstairs to tell Peyton that Laurissa was here, only to see her bent over in a position that should probably be illegal. He thought he might have to jump in the ocean for a while to cool off.

That had been over three hours ago. Laurissa had long since gone and Peyton had taken her sexy yoga pants and even sexier butt back upstairs to get some more writing done. The scary part was that even now he couldn't get the image out of his head. It was possible the sight had been permanently burned into his mind.

Noah went back to reading Peyton's book. Or at least tried to. Mostly, he sat there on the couch wondering what it was about her that had him so off balance. It wasn't like he'd never been around a beautiful woman before. He had. Lots of them. But there was something about her that got to him.

The crazy part of it was that Peyton wasn't really the type Noah normally dated. He'd never given much thought about his type before, but he realized he tended to go after women who were outgoing to the point of being loud. Like the kind of woman you'd pick up in a club—or one who might pick him up.

Peyton wasn't that kind of woman. He'd met her less than twenty-four hours ago, but he already knew that much about her. Yet, he was fascinated by her. Her quiet sensuality, the way she seemed surprised by how sexy she was, the blush that tinted her skin every now and then. Things he'd never imagined being attracted to, were the things knocking him off his feet and telling him to try someone who wasn't his type at all. Someone unique. Someone he might actually consider having a long-term relationship with.

Someone who was depending on him to keep her safe.

Someone he was sure who wasn't looking for her bodyguard to make a move on her.

The power dynamics alone made the situation nearly untenable.

On top of that, there was the whole Navy SEAL thing. He'd dated lots of women who were intrigued at the idea of being with a SEAL. They liked the visual of having a boyfriend in a dangerous line of work. But in his experience, that thrill rarely kept them around for long. Having a boyfriend disappear without notice, missing dates, birthdays, dinners with friends and family without ever being told where he'd gone was stuff few women could put up with for long. He doubted Peyton would be any different.

Noah leaned forward, dropping the book on the table and reaching for his mug of coffee, shaking his head when he realized it was empty. He'd been so busy thinking about Peyton, he didn't even remember drinking it.

He was heading for the kitchen when he heard a thud from upstairs. He stopped in midstride, tensing. Then he relaxed again. There was no way someone could get in the house without him knowing. Even if they could, he doubted they'd be ballsy enough to do it in the middle of the afternoon. Peyton had probably dropped something.

He made it all the way to the fridge this time before he heard another thud, louder this time. Okay, maybe he should go check on her.

Noah jogged up the stairs, taking them two at a time until he felt a little twinge in his knee, which made him slow down. But he still moved as quickly as he could, making his way silently down the hall to her office. For the second time that day, he stopped in the doorway and stared transfixed.

Peyton was dancing around the room in shorts and a tank top, her feet bare, her iPhone in her hand, buds in her ears, and her back to him. Noah thought the yoga pose he'd seen her in that morning was sexy, but watching her hips wiggle to whatever music she was listening to was hot enough to make him go hard in his jeans.

Noah knew he should go back downstairs. Peyton wasn't in danger. If anything, he was the one at risk here. Watching her shake that cute little butt was damn near killing him.

Besides, if he left now, she'd never know he was standing here like some kinky voyeur.

But then Peyton twirled around to face him.

She jumped, her eyes going wide. Color crept into her cheeks as she yanked the buds from her ears.

"I didn't mean to startle you," he said. "I heard noise and came up to check on you."

"Oh."

She transferred her phone and buds to one hand, then reached up with the other to tuck her long hair behind her ear. Noah wondered if it felt as silky as it looked. The urge to find out was so strong he had to shove his hands in the front pockets of his jeans so he wouldn't do something crazy.

Peyton gave him an embarrassed look. "Sometimes when the words aren't coming as fast as I'd like, I get up and dance. Sorry I worried you by making so much noise."

"Don't be sorry," he said. "You dance great."

She blushed again, deeper this time. "Now you're making fun of me."

He shook his head. "No, I'm not. You have some serious moves."

She ducked her head a little "Thank you."

With the apologies and compliments out of the way, Noah told himself he should go downstairs, but he couldn't make himself move. That probably had something to do with the way

Peyton was standing there gazing into his eyes, her lips slightly parted, her face still flushed.

He wasn't even sure how many times his phone rang before he realized what the hell was making so much noise.

Shit.

Noah dug his phone out of his pocket and put it to his ear without even checking to see who it was. "Bradley."

"Noah, thank God you answered!"

His hand tightened reflexively on the phone, his heart beginning to speed up at the anxiety in his mother's voice. "Mom, calm down. What's wrong?"

"The sink in the kitchen started leaking and I'm afraid it's going to flood the whole house," his mother said in a panicked voice. "Can you come over and fix it? And don't say you're working because I know you're still on medical leave."

Noah glanced at Peyton with a frown. She was regarding him curiously, concern in her blue eyes. "Yeah, I'm on medical leave, but that doesn't mean I'm not working. I'm doing something important right now and I can't just up and leave. You're going to have to call a plumber."

"A plumber?" His mother sighed. "You know

how long it takes to get anyone to show up in this town. What am I supposed to do until they get here? Why can't you come over? What are you doing that's so important?"

"I'm doing some work on the side while my knee heals up and I can't get away right now," he said again, kind of shocked Laurissa hadn't already told their mom about the bodyguard gig. "If you're worried about the house flooding, turn off the water."

"You know I don't know how to do that." Another sigh. "Fine. If it floods the house, it floods the house. But if I drown, it will be your fault."

It was Noah's turn to sigh. Sometimes his mother was a complete drama llama. "Mom, it's not going to flood the house and you're not going to drown. Now, I have to go. I'll call to check on you later, okay?"

"What was all that about?" Peyton asked as he hung up.

Noah quickly filled in the parts of the conversation she hadn't heard.

Peyton frowned. "Your mom's right. It could take hours for a plumber to show up. Besides, they'll charge a fortune. It's silly for her to pay all that money if you can fix it." She eyed him. "You can fix it, right?"

"Probably, but—"

"Then it's settled. Call and tell her we'll come right over."

He lifted a brow. "We will?"

Peyton nodded. "You said you go where I go, right? That means I have to go with you."

"What about your writing?"

She made a face. "I'm stuck anyway. That's why I was dancing around before, remember? Getting away from the keyboard for a while will help. Call your mom while I go change."

Noah opened his mouth to stop her, but she'd already left the room. Damn, it seemed Peyton could be a force of nature when she wanted to be. Shaking his head, he took out his phone and called his mom—who was thrilled to hear he was coming—then went downstairs to wait for Peyton.

She came down ten minutes later dressed in a long, flowy, colorful skirt and sleeveless top. Damn, she made Boho look awesome!

"Do you have your hard drive?" he asked as he held the door open.

She patted the huge purse she had slung over

one shoulder. "It's like that credit card commercial. I never leave home without it."

Crap, between her coming with him to his mother's house and him making sure she had her book with her, it was like they were a couple.

As they walked to his SUV, Noah automatically checked the area for threats. He didn't expect anyone to try anything with him there, but years of training and instincts couldn't be ignored.

He glanced at Peyton as he backed out of the driveway. "Thanks."

"For what?"

"Running over to my mom's with me. I promise I'll fix the sink as quickly as I can."

"Don't worry about it," Peyton said. "I've loved your mom from the moment Laurissa introduced us at our first parents' weekend in college."

Noah felt a smile tug at the corners of his mouth. "Sounds about right. Everyone who's ever met my mom falls in love with her."

Peyton laughed. "Which is why I'm at her house so much with your sister. Which makes me wonder how it is that I've never met you in person before now."

He winced. He already felt crappy enough about not visiting his mother very often, especially since he certainly lived close enough. "I know I don't get over there as much as I should, but with my job, it's tough. I'm either gone on missions, training, or too worn out to even want to leave my apartment."

"I guess riding sharks while chasing nuclear submarines can be exhausting," she said.

"Riding sharks?" Noah kept one eye on the road while glancing over at Peyton, sure he must have heard her wrong. "What are you talking about?"

Peyton laughed. "It was just something Laurissa said yesterday about the kind of stuff you do in the SEALs."

Noah could definitely believe his sister saying something like that, mostly because he never told her anything about what he did for a living. His mom and sister worried about him enough. "I've done some crazy things as a SEAL, but I'm pretty sure I've never ridden a shark. I think I'd remember that."

"I think she got you confused with Aquaman." Peyton laughed again, then regarded him thoughtfully. "What made you join the Navy and become a SEAL?"

Noah opened his mouth, intending to give

Peyton the standard line about wanting to serve his country and patriotism. But while both of those things *had* played a part in him joining the Navy, they weren't the deciding factors. And for some reason, he wanted her to know the real reason he did.

"Did Laurissa tell you about our dad bailing on us when we were kids?"

She nodded.

"The part Laurissa probably didn't know is that he took everything he and my mom had in savings when he left." Noah tightened his hold on the wheel. Just thinking about it pissed him off. "Mom worked double shifts at the hospital where she was a nurse to make ends meet, but with no child support, we weren't in the best of situations. She did her best not to let any of it affect us, saying it was her responsibility to take care of us. She wouldn't even let me get a part-time job to help out until I was seventeen. She was too afraid it'd interfere with school."

"Wow." Peyton shook her head. "I always knew your mom was awesome, but I think I underestimated her."

Noah chuckled. "Yeah, she's all that and a bag of chips. But no matter how great my mom is or how hard she worked, she couldn't replace all the money my dad took. Something had to be sacrificed and that something was our college fund. There simply wasn't enough to send two people to school. Hell, there wasn't enough to send one."

Peyton looked at him like he was the fuzziest puppy in the litter. "You went in the Navy so Laurissa would have money to go to school? That's so sweet I want to hug the stuffing out of you."

He shrugged, thinking he might like getting hugged like that. Especially if she was the one doing the hugging. "I have to admit, the move wasn't completely altruistic. Truthfully, when I graduated high school, college would have been a waste for me. My head wasn't in the right place for it. The military seemed like a more logical choice at the time, so I went to a recruiter and, as the saying goes, the rest is history."

"Why the Navy?"

"My grandfather was in the Navy," he said. "He'd tell me stories all the time about it when I was a kid, so I didn't have to think too hard about which branch of service I wanted to join. My grandfather would never have let me live it down if I joined any of the others."

She smiled. “I bet your grandfather was very proud when he saw you in your uniform the first time.”

“He was. He passed away shortly after that.” Noah swallowed hard. “But at least he was able to see me graduate BUD/S—Basic Underwater Demolition/SEAL training,” he added, knowing Peyton would have no clue what the acronym stood for.

“I’m sorry,” she said quietly. “You sound like you miss him very much.”

“Yeah. He was more of a dad to me than my real father ever was, even before he walked out.”

He’d never told anyone that, not even his mom, but it was true.

“Was he a SEAL, too?”

Noah shook his head. “No, he wasn’t a SEAL. He spent his entire career in the Navy working on communication and radar equipment.”

“So, if it wasn’t for your grandfather, why go into the SEALs?”

He gave her a small smile. “I wish I had a simple answer for you. All I can really say is that I was a little lost back then and looking for something to give me purpose...a challenge. I’d always been athletic and loved the water, so when the recruiter showed me a video of all the cool stuff SEALs did, I couldn't sign up fast enough."

Peyton snorted. "Hence the reason they show those videos to eighteen-year-old kids in the first place. What teenager doesn't want to have a job where he gets to be a badass?"

"True that," he laughed. "I barely had a clue what I was getting into and never cared for a second."

"I'm sure you didn't," Peyton said. "But what did your mom think of it? From what I've heard, SEALs do dangerous stuff and are always off in the farthest corners of the world."

He grimaced as he remembered that particular conversation with his mother. "She didn't think much of it, that's for sure. She worries about me at the best of times. Knowing I would be doing a dangerous job only made her worry more. It doesn't help that I can't tell her about where I'm going when I leave. Her imagination runs wild, which is the worst possible thing."

"I can certainly understand that," she said softly. "Having the people we love in danger is always hard, but not knowing whether they're in danger or not would be even more horrible."

That was true, but there wasn't anything he

could do about it. Besides the whole issue of all his missions being classified out the whazoo, his family would probably be even more freaked out if they knew what kind of stuff he did when he was out of the country. Like nearly twisting his leg off in Yemen.

They drove for a while in silence, a part of Noah wanting to ask if Peyton would worry about him as much as his family did. But he kept the question to himself, not wanting to ruin the mood any more than it already was.

"Do you ever see your father?" she asked suddenly, apparently deciding to change the topic of conversation in lieu of continuing the silence.

Noah tightened his grip on the wheel again. The subject of his dad had always been a sore one, even after all this time. "Not since he walked out on us fourteen years ago. Last I heard, he was shacked up with some woman in Vegas, making a living as an Elvis impersonator."

"Do you hate him for leaving?" Peyton asked quietly, an understanding expression on her face. "I don't think anyone would blame you if you did. I know I probably would."

Noah thought about that question for a moment before answering, realizing it was another subject he'd never talked about with anyone. Funny how he seemed to be able to do it with someone he'd just met.

"I did at first, mostly for what his leaving did to Mom and my sister," he said, hesitating as he turned the vehicle into the subdivision his mom had lived in for as long as Noah could remember. "But not so much now. We've all moved on without him, and these days I can't muster up much of any emotion when it comes to the man."

Peyton nodded but didn't say anything. Not that there was anything that needed to be said. He'd talked more about himself in the past few minutes than he had in the last ten years. He blamed it on Peyton and those books of hers he'd been reading. The hero in those stories always seemed to be sharing his feelings, which confirmed beyond all shadow of a doubt that they were works of fiction. He'd been in a platoon full of SEALs for years and even in all that time, he'd have a hard time filling a thimble with the collective outpouring of the guys' emotions. Because they basically didn't do it.

Peyton was obviously a bad influence on him. Or at least her books were.

Noah pulled into the driveway of the

two-story house he still considered home. It looked no different than it had ten years ago when he joined the Navy, with the exception of the new roof and the fresh coat of paint he'd put on not that long ago. There were a bunch of newly planted flowers in the front beds as well, something his mom loved doing. As much as he'd loved moving out and being on his own, it was always nice to come back here.

"Well," he said as he turned off the engine and opened his door, "you ready to save my mom from drowning?"

CHAPTER

PEYTON HALF EXPECTED TO HEAR THE SOUND OF rushing water when she stepped through the front door of Eileen's home, or worse, see signs of it running across the floor. But as she looked across the living room and into the kitchen beyond, there wasn't a single sign of flooding.

But there also wasn't any sign of Eileen. And that worried Peyton more than a little. If the expression on Noah's face was any indication, so was he.

"Mom," he called out, moving the small bag of tools he'd taken from behind the seat of his SUV to his other hand before turning toward the kitchen. "Are you in here?"

"In the laundry room!" Eileen's familiar voice came from somewhere nearby.

Noah gestured for Peyton to go ahead of

him, following close behind as they entered the country style kitchen that was so warm and inviting. Exactly like Noah's mom. There was a crock-pot simmering on the counter near the stove, the delicious aroma of whatever was in it filling the room. Peyton couldn't help but imagine Noah and Laurissa running around in here when they were younger. She found herself smiling at the thought.

"I wanted to have more towels handy in case the pipe burst," the petite woman with shoulder-length blond hair said as she walked into the kitchen with a big stack of bath towels in her arms. When she caught sight of Peyton, she stopped and stared, clearly surprised to see her. Eileen's gaze drifted to Noah before going back to her. "Peyton! What are you doing here?"

Peyton smiled. "It's a long, complicated story that we'll tell you all about, but first, maybe we should let Noah deal with the leak."

Eileen seemed like she would have preferred to hear that story, but finally hurried over to the kitchen table to put the stack of towels down. Then she reached out to give Peyton a big hug, her eyes darting back and forth between the two of them again, her expression a cross between curious and suspicious. "Okay. But if I find out you and Noah have been dating without telling me anything about it, I'm going to be mad!"

Noah's eyes widened and he did a double take, clearly stunned at the direction his mom's imagination had taken her. Which he shouldn't be, since Eileen was always trying to play matchmaker.

"Whoa, Mom, slow down." He held up his hands in a gesture of surrender. "Peyton's not my girlfriend. I'm her bodyguard."

Peyton sighed. No way was Eileen going to let that go. So much for fixing the leak first.

Eileen's gaze rested on Noah for a few moments before moving to Peyton and then back again, her face filled with disappointment, like she honestly had been hoping they were together. Which was silly. His mother had to realize she and Noah were way too different for that.

"Sorry for jumping to conclusions," Eileen said, offering Peyton a small smile before her expression turned serious again. "But why do you need a bodyguard?"

Peyton started to answer but was interrupted as Noah stepped forward. "Mom, like Peyton said, we'll tell you everything, but why don't you show me the leak first? Before any of us drown, remember?"

The comment about drowning seemed to finally get through to his mother and Eileen snapped out of matchmaking mode only to go into a long explanation about how she'd come home from work to a dripping faucet and water pouring out of the cabinet under the sink.

Noah dropped his bag of tools on the tile floor and crouched down to open the cabinet and take a look under the sink. He'd barely gotten started when the front door banged open and Laurissa came storming into the kitchen followed by a tall woman in her mid-twenties with long, dark hair.

"I don't have a clue what to do with a leaky sink, so I brought Tabitha with me for backup," Laurissa said. "She's totally into mechanical stuff."

Laurissa chose that moment to notice there was someone else in the kitchen besides her mom, looking at Peyton in confusion for a second before glancing down at her brother leaning halfway into the cabinet under the sink. "Peyton? What are you guys doing here? Or more precisely, if Noah is here, why am I? He can obviously fix a leaky sink better than I can."

"I called your brother first, but he claimed he was too busy working so I called you," Eileen said. "Then a few minutes later, Noah called back, saying he'd changed his mind. I tried to reach you to say you didn't have to come, but you never answered the phone. As far as Peyton, I'm as surprised to see her as you are. I wasn't even aware they knew each other."

Noah hadn't bothered to crawl out of the cabinet, so Peyton figured it was left to her to explain what was going on. But then she caught sight of Tabitha staring at her with eyes as wide as saucers, face flushing like she was about to pass out.

"Oh. My. God," the woman breathed. "You're Peyton Matthews. *The* Peyton Matthews. You're real." She shot Laurissa an accusing look. "Some friend you are! Why didn't you tell me you knew Peyton Matthews and that your brother is dating her?"

There was a loud thud from under the sink, immediately followed by a muttered curse. "Why does everyone think we're dating?" he called out while continuing to work on the pipes under there. "Do I have a sign hanging around my neck or something?"

Peyton laughed, wondering for the second

time why anyone would think that she and Noah would make a good couple. It was ludicrous.

"Yes, I know Peyton Matthews. We've been friends since college," Laurissa said. "I never told you because it never came up in conversation. It's not exactly something you slip into the middle of our morning rant on *The Bachelor*. And no, my brother isn't dating her. He's her bodyguard."

"You knew about this and didn't tell me?" Eileen said, her expression changing from the surprise and confusion she'd displayed the first time around to something closer to downright irritation. "Why am I the last one to know?"

Ignoring both Laurissa and her mother, Peyton stepped forward to introduce herself to Tabitha, who was still staring at her with huge eyes, hoping that would forestall more conversation on why she needed a bodyguard. "Hi! You already know who I am, but to make it official, I'm Peyton. Nice to meet you."

"This is my friend from work, Tabitha Turner," Laurissa said when Tabitha only continued to stare.

"I absolutely love, love, love your books!" Tabitha finally managed, bouncing up and down excitedly.

Peyton laughed. It would be disconcerting if she wasn't already used to fans doing it. She immediately went into author mode, asking Tabitha which books were her favorite and which characters she liked the most. Before long, Tabitha—and Laurissa—were rattling off titles and talking about the characters like they were real people. Which they were for most fans.

By the time Noah appeared from under the sink, apparently done with the leak, Peyton, Laurissa, and Tabitha were busy taking selfies with each other.

"I know you guys will tag me, but let me get some with my phone, too," Peyton said, grabbing her purse. She rummaged through it for a moment, frowning when she couldn't find it. "Well, crap. I hope I didn't leave it somewhere. I'm always doing that." She looked at Noah. "Can I use your phone to take the picture?"

"Yeah, sure."

He pulled his cell out of his pocket and handed it to her, then started putting his tools away in his bag. From the corner of her eye, she could see him looking her way as she snapped a few photos of herself, Laurissa, and Tabitha. When she was finished, she quickly emailed herself the photos.

Then, figuring he wouldn't mind, she quickly downloaded the Find My Phone app. A moment later, a map came up on the screen.

"Just as I thought." She handed the phone back to him with a smile. "I left my cell at home. Sometimes I think I'd leave my head behind if it wasn't attached. Everything good with the leak?"

"The threat of everyone drowning has been neutralized," he said with a laugh as he wiped his hands on one of the towels Eileen has left on the table. "Just had to tighten the nut on the shutoff valve. Give me a minute or two to get everything cleaned up and we can get out of here."

Peyton had absolutely no idea what Noah was taking about when it came to the plumbing, but she recognized he wanted to bail before his mom could ask too many questions. Unfortunately, Eileen picked up on that plan as quickly as Peyton did.

"Noah, you and Peyton must stay for dinner," his mother said. "I have a crockpot full of white chili and there's more there than I could ever eat. Laurissa, you and Tabitha stay as well. It's been a while since we've all been together for a meal."

Peyton certainly wouldn't mind some of Eileen's famous chili, but a covert glance in Noah's direction showed him shaking his head, obviously not wanting to hang around to be cross examined by his mother.

"Thanks, Mom, but—" he began, only to have Tabitha of all people cut him off.

"Noah, you and Peyton *have* to stay," Laurissa's friend said imploringly. "Please say you'll stay for dinner. I have so much I want to talk to Peyton about."

Noah glanced at Peyton, who eagerly nodded, before turning to his mother. "Okay, we'll stay. If you're sure it isn't any trouble."

His mother smiled broadly. "It's no trouble at all. Go put those tools away and wash up. Laurissa, can you and Tabitha please set the table while Peyton helps me make some cornbread?"

Peyton had to bite her tongue to keep from laughing as Noah walked away to clean up, looking for all the world like he expected nothing but trouble out of this evening.

She'd seen Eileen cook dinner plenty of times but was still amazed at how fast the woman got a big sheet of cornbread drop biscuits into the oven. Peyton was supposed to be helping, but she didn't do much more than measure a few ingredients and stir when Eileen instructed.

While Laurissa and Tabitha set the table, and the cornbread baked, Eileen busied herself with adding a few extra spices to the crockpot. The smell was incredible, and Peyton would have been jealous of Eileen's skills in the kitchen if she didn't get a chance to eat her food so often.

"So, how long has Noah been staying at your place?" Eileen asked softly as she stirred a little more cumin into the chili.

"Since last night. The publisher wants him to stay until the next book is turned in, so at least two weeks. Maybe more."

Peyton wasn't sure where Eileen was going with this and wondered if maybe she should wait until Noah was with her before saying anything more.

"Two weeks." Eileen glanced at her. "That's a long time to have somebody you don't know hanging around your house. I guess that means you're comfortable having him around?"

"Oh, yes!" That was louder than she intended, giving the way Laurissa and Tabitha suddenly looked over. "I mean, he's easy to be around," she added in a softer voice. "He makes me feel safe. I've definitely slept better than I have in a while, especially considering the stress I'm under with this deadline."

"It probably helps that he's not hard to look at," Eileen murmured casually, throwing a pinch of salt in the crockpot and mixing it in.

Peyton felt her face heat. She opened her mouth to deny everything, but the words wouldn't come. "I suppose I'd be lying if I said looking at him was a hardship. Your son is sinfully attractive."

She blushed even more. Had those words really just come out of her mouth? This was Noah's mom she was talking to!

"You'd be good for him." Eileen gave the chili one more stir, then placed the lid back on the pot. "He needs someone like you in his life, even if he doesn't know it yet. Being with a SEAL isn't easy, but something tells me that you can handle it."

Peyton froze. Crap, this conversation had suddenly gotten very serious, very quickly. She started to say things weren't moving anywhere in that direction, but the expression on Eileen's face stopped her.

"Are you in danger?" Eileen asked softly, throwing a quick look at Laurissa and Tabitha before lowering her voice even more. "Is that why Noah didn't want to stay over for dinner?"

Peyton glanced at Tabitha. She liked to think

Tabitha wouldn't spread anything she heard here tonight, but none of this was stuff her publisher would want to get out to the general public. Before she could figure out how to answer the question, Noah was at her side, eyeing the two of them suspiciously, as if he'd somehow known they were talking about something serious.

"Your mom wants to know if I'm in danger," Peyton said softly. "And I thought you'd rather tell her the story now, instead of while we're eating dinner with Tabitha."

"I'd rather not tell her at all," Noah said shortly. "But since I know she won't stop badgering us if I don't, I guess I don't have a whole lot of choice."

Eileen laughed as she turned the light on in the oven and bent down to check on the cornbread through the window. "That's true."

Peyton mostly listened as Noah quickly explained the situation, only adding details when Eileen specifically asked for them. She didn't want to worry Noah's mother, but the longer they talked, the more concerned Eileen looked.

"Is it safe at your house?" Eileen asked softly, pulling the cornbread out and transferring the little biscuits to a serving basket. "Would it be better if the two of you stayed here with me?"

Noah frowned. "Thanks for the offer, Mom. Really. But if I thought I couldn't keep Peyton safe at her place, I definitely wouldn't bring her here and put you at risk, too. If we need to go somewhere else, it'll be to a place no one can get near her, much less find her."

From the look on Eileen's face, it was obvious she didn't like that idea at all. But she bit her tongue and nodded, then headed toward the table with the cornbread, motioning at Noah to bring the chili.

He took the ceramic pot from its heating element, glancing at Peyton as he set it on a metal trey in the shape of a chicken. "Hope I didn't scare you with all that talk of moving you to someplace you couldn't be found. I would never do that unless I really had to, if it means keeping you safe."

She reached out and put her hand on his arm, feeling the corded muscles beneath her fingers. It was difficult to describe the comfort she felt having him this close. "You didn't scare me. The opposite in fact. It's nice knowing I have somebody who'd do anything necessary to keep me safe."

He gazed down at her warmly, and for a moment, Peyton thought he was going to kiss her. And despite the belief that they were two different to ever get together, she was more than ready to let him. Even if it was right in the middle of his mom's kitchen.

But then Laurissa and Tabitha were calling out from the table, telling them to hurry up with the food, and the moment was gone.

"You ready to have dinner with Tabitha, the super fan?" Noah asked, a grin replacing the intense look that had been there mere seconds before as he picked up the tray. "Something tells me she's going to talk your ear off tonight."

Peyton laughed. "I'm not too worried about that. There's a reason I have two of them."

CHAPTER *Six*

IT WAS WELL AFTER TEN BY THE TIME NOAH PULLED HIS SUV into the driveway of Peyton's home and turned off the engine. It was only then that he realized how tired he was. And that his ears were actually ringing a little bit. Turns out Tabitha could be really loud when she was excited about something.

"Are all fans like that?" he asked as they sat there in the vehicle.

Peyton leaned back in her seat, stretching like a cat. "Like what?"

He grinned. "As intense as Tabitha. I'm surprised you had a chance to eat, the way she kept bombarding you with questions."

"Oh!" Peyton laughed. "Most of them are exactly like that. But those are the best kind of fans. I love meeting people like Tabitha, people who are as excited about my characters as I am. It lets me know they're invested completely in the story, and that's what it's all about."

He gave her a sidelong glance, his hands still resting on the steering wheel. "But it's a story. They know that, right?"

"Sure. But the very best books are those that grab the readers and pull them in anyway. It gives them characters they care about and fall in love with. It's a total escape from the rest of the world."

Noah considered that. When Peyton put it that way, he supposed it made sense. Tabitha had looked like it was Christmas morning when she'd recognized Peyton standing in the kitchen. And even Laurissa's eyes had been shining bright as the three of them talked about the characters and plot lines in Peyton's books. Hell, even his mom joined in a few times, which shocked the crap out of Noah. He had no idea she even read, much less books about young adults. He found himself smiling at the thought. The whole evening had definitely been a learning experience, but he had to admit he enjoyed himself.

In the beginning, he'd been half afraid his mother would pull out photos of him as a baby or something equally horrifying. But thankfully, she was on her best behavior. Just as importantly, she also didn't bring up the topic of Peyton being in danger or Noah being her bodyguard. That was something he didn't want to discuss in front of Tabitha.

Instead, Tabitha begged for spoilers about what was going to happen next in the series. Spoilers that Peyton refused to give her. Laurissa's friend had been totally bummed by that until Peyton promised to get her into the release party on Saturday and a signed copy of the new book coming out. Tabitha pretty much lost her mind. Five minutes later, she was on her phone excitedly texting all her friends. He guessed it didn't take much to make a super fan happy.

"Come on. Time to get you inside."

Stepping out of the SUV, he quickly walked around to open the passenger door before she could do it herself. Not only did he like being a gentleman, but he didn't want her outside by herself with him on the other side of the vehicle. The chances of there being someone lurking around waiting for a moment like that was slim, but he wasn't ready to take any chances.

"Stay here while I check the rest of the house," he said once they were in the living room with the front door locked and all the first-floor lights on. The look Peyton gave him told him she didn't think it was necessary, but she didn't say anything as he headed up the stairs.

He checked each room quickly, slipping from Peyton's bedroom to the guest room, workout room, then finishing up with the home office. Her laptop was exactly where she'd left it and there wasn't any indication that anything had been touched.

As he headed down the stairs, Noah replayed the conversation he had with his mom before they left. The one where she'd once again tried her hand at playing matchmaker.

"Peyton is a very attractive woman," his mom had pointed out while filling a plastic container with leftover chili for them. "She has a good head on her shoulders, too. You could do worse."

Noah sighed. "That's all true, but right now, she's depending on me to keep her safe. That's what I'm focused on."

"As you should be," his mother agreed. "But this bodyguard thing isn't going to last forever. When she's safe, there's no reason you can't continue to see her. Unless you're worried about there being some other man in her life."

He couldn't help but chuckle as he took the container from his mom, wondering if she already knew the answer to that. "Peyton doesn't have a boyfriend."

His mother beamed. "I knew you liked her. And don't try to deny it. If you didn't like her, you wouldn't bother finding out if she had a boyfriend or not. So, when this is situation is taken care of, I'll be expecting to see you two spending time together."

Noah had opened his mouth to tell his mother there was no reason to assume Peyton had any interest in a man whose job pulled him off to one hellhole after another with little or no warning, but before he got the words out, she walked away, leaving him with nothing to do but to shake his head in amusement at how simple she made the world out to be sometimes.

When he got downstairs, Noah found Peyton standing in the living room in the same exact spot he'd left her.

"Everything looks good," he said.

Peyton might like to claim she wasn't in any danger, but there was no mistaking the relief in her eyes.

"I should get to bed then," she said. "I had a great time tonight."

"Me, too," he said, and realized he meant it.

Best damn date-that-wasn't-a-date he'd ever been on.

Noah watched Peyton disappear upstairs, then took a quick walk around the property outside before coming back in to check the doors and windows. Then he grabbed his toiletry kit from his bag over behind the couch, dropped his phone, wallet, and keys on the coffee table and headed for the downstairs bathroom. Slipping inside, he left the door open just enough to be able to hear anything while he showered, then took off his clothes. He stepped into the shower just as the water turned on upstairs.

The thought of Peyton standing naked in the shower had his cock springing to attention. He groaned and reached for the all-in-one shampoo/shower gel he'd brought from home, then squeezed some into his hand and lathered it fiercely into his hair, hoping it would get the image of a very sexy, very naked Peyton out of his head.

It didn't help.

As the suds ran down his chest, he imagined Peyton standing in the shower with him so close they were almost touching. He pictured her creamy skin slick with water, her nipples peeking out through the soap bubbles. In his mind's eye, he cupped her breasts, wiping the foam away with his thumbs and revealing the rosy tips underneath to give them a squeeze. In the fantasy, his hands moved downward, gliding over her hips and around to cup that perfect butt so he could get a grip and pull her against him. From there, he could do so many things.

He could slip one hand between her legs and caress her until she screamed his name. Or he could lift her up and plunge inside her while she wrapped her legs around his waist. Or he could turn her around and bend her over just enough to take her from behind.

The possibilities were limited only by his imagination, and while he might not be a writer, he had a very good imagination when it came to making love to beautiful women.

His shaft throbbed between his legs, sending a tremor through him.

Noah cursed and rinsed the last of the soap away, then turned off the hot water and turned on the cold full force, gritting his teeth as the icy spray washed over his body.

An hour ago, he'd been telling his mother he

couldn't think about anything but keeping Peyton safe. So why was he torturing himself with fantasies of something he couldn't have? Maybe because he was a glutton for punishment.

Turning off the water, he climbed out of the shower and grabbed a towel from the rack. He dried off, then wrapped the towel around his waist and pushed open the partially closed door only to walk right into Peyton when he stepped into the hallway. She was wearing a tiny pair of shorts and a tank top that cupped her breasts the same way he'd imagined his hands doing earlier. He swallowed hard and tried not to look at all that expanse of skin.

He mumbled something he hoped sounded intelligible and moved to step around her as Peyton did the same. Their feet tangled and she stumbled. He caught her arms to steady her at the same time she put her hands on his bare chest. She gazed up at him with mesmerizing eyes, her lips parting ever so slightly.

Before he could even process why this wasn't a good idea, he bent his head and kissed her. Her lips were soft and sweet under his, and he buried his fingers in her long hair, wanting—needing—more. She tasted like minty toothpaste and strawberries, and the combination almost brought him to his knees.

Peyton moaned against his mouth, gliding her hands up his chest to grip his shoulders and hold on tight as she kissed him back. The realization she wanted him as much as he wanted her was like an intoxicating drug sending desire surging through his blood, and he let out a groan of his own as her tongue played a sexy game of hide-and-seek with his.

Under the towel, his cock pitched a tent, all set to make camp for the night.

Noah was sliding his other hand down to cup her ass so he could pull her closer when a high-pitched noise filled the house. It took him a minute to realize it was his cell phone ringing. As much as he wanted to say the hell with it, years of being a SEAL made him drag his mouth away from Peyton's. Business before pleasure.

"I have to get that."

She pulled back, looking a tad bit dazed as she nodded her head, even swaying a little on her feet as he hurried into the living room to grab his phone off the coffee table where he'd left it earlier.

"Bradley," he said without looking at the

name on the screen, too focused on getting his breathing back under control.

"Hey, Noah, it's Sam. I didn't wake you up, did I?"

Noah cleared his throat as he looked down at the towel covering his crotch and almost laughed. "No. What's up?"

Your cock, a smartass voice sounded off in his head. Fortunately, that voice wasn't capable of talking to his Teammate at the moment.

"We just sat through another intel brief with Agent Woods," Sam said. "He said some stuff I thought you might want to know about. Nothing earth shattering, but definitely interesting."

Noah took a deep breath and let it out slowly, using the distraction of Sam's voice to get himself back under control. He was only partially successful, but at least his bath towel wasn't tenting as badly as before.

"According to Woods, Magpie and his organization are under tremendous pressure to come through with alternative sources of funding for their terrorist network. We're talking huge amounts of money in a very short period of time. If he doesn't come up with it, he may not live long enough to regret it."

Noah snorted. "I guess the world of terrorists is one of those what-have-you-done-for-me lately kind of deals. Does Woods think you guys will get called out to go after him soon?"

There was a moment of hesitation before Sam answered. "Actually, Woods thinks Magpie might be somewhere in the U.S. involved personally in a quick score to get the heat off himself."

It took less than a second for the implications of Sam's words to sink in. Noah suddenly understood exactly why his buddy had called so late. He tried to tell himself the odds Magpie was here in southern California were slim. Somewhere in the U.S. wasn't exactly very definitive and there were thousands of other places the man could go looking for a quick score.

Still, Sam was calling for a reason.

"You think Magpie may have been behind the break-in at Peyton's house, don't you?" Noah asked, praying he was wrong.

There was another long pause. "I don't know, but as soon as Woods said that crap about Magpie possibly being in the country, Wes and Lane both looked at me. We were all thinking the same thing. And you were the one who pointed out how much money her book would be worth on the open market. Something like that might be enough to draw Magpie out of hiding."

"You didn't say anything about this to Woods, did you?" Noah asked.

He wasn't sure if he was more worried about the information getting back to Chasen and headquarters or because they wouldn't let him keep protecting Peyton.

"No way," Sam said. "Not on just a hunch. And not when you're personally invested in keeping Peyton safe."

He was tempted to say it wasn't like that, to insist there was no personal investment. But the kiss that had happened a few minutes ago made that a lie.

"But just because we didn't say anything doesn't mean you shouldn't be extra careful," Sam added. "The second you get the slightest hint this is anything more than some random book thief, call us for backup, okay?"

After promising he'd call if anything happened and making sure Sam would let him know if anything more definitive turned up with Magpie, Noah hung up. Then he stood there, worrying what the hell he should do next.

There was a part of him—located south of his

belly button—that urged him to run after Peyton and get back to what they'd been doing a little while ago. Preferably on the nearest horizontal surface. But at the same time, a more intelligent part suggested that maybe he needed to slow down a little. Some of it had to do with this latest concern over Magpie and that the man might be behind the effort to steal Peyton's book. If so, he'd try again and would likely stop at nothing to get what he wanted. Violence was a given.

But while Noah accepted that getting sexually—and probably emotionally—involved with the woman you were trying to keep safe wasn't the brightest idea, he also accepted that wasn't the thing making him hesitate at the moment. As insane as it sounded, there was something else going on between him and Peyton. Something he didn't want to screw up. For the first time ever, he found himself wanting more from a woman than a good time. It was one of those stop-the-presses kind of moment. He liked Peyton—a lot—and he couldn't help but wonder if that meant he needed to take things slowly with her.

He found Peyton standing at the counter in the kitchen, her back to him as she squirted whipped cream into two mugs of hot chocolate. He stopped, watching her from behind as she worked. The sight of those sexy little shorts and the tank top bunched up just enough to reveal a little glimpse of skin at her waist almost made him groan. It was scary that he could be so attracted and aroused by a simple flash of flesh like that. The urge to step forward and run his fingers across that tiny sliver of perfection was damn near impossible to resist.

But he did. Because he wanted this to work out. And he doubted it would if they ended up naked on the kitchen floor.

"Sprinkles?" she asked suddenly.

Noah looked up to see her looking at him over her shoulder, her eyes warm and playful. The smile curving her lips was sensual, making him question his decision-making process.

"In your cocoa," she added.

He jerked his gaze from those sinful lips down to the mugs, trying to comprehend what the hell she was talking about. It took a second for his mind to recalibrate and finally notice the little plastic shaker bottle of chocolate flakes in her hand.

"No. Thanks," he finally managed to answer. "I prefer my hot chocolate straight."

Peyton laughed, taking a moment to shake a few of the chocolate sprinkles onto the top of one of the whipped cream covered mugs of cocoa before handing him the other one. She took a quick sip, leaving the most adorable trace of cream on her upper lip.

Regardless of his earlier plan, he didn't try and stop himself. He merely set his cocoa on the counter and bent his head to swipe the whipped cream away with his tongue. The taste was so sweet he groaned out loud. And the delicious favor had absolutely nothing to do with the topping.

Peyton's mug joined his on the counter and then her arms were around his neck, dragging him down for a deeper kiss.

The sounds she made as they kissed, the feel of her breasts pressing against his chest through the thin material of her tank top, and the wiggle of her tongue had Noah hard as a rock all over again and ready to tear the towel aside and take her right there in the kitchen.

That's why he broke the kiss and stepped back.

Seeing the confusion and disappointment on Peyton's face was a like a punch to the gut, but he took a deep breath and steeled himself.

You're a SEAL, dammit. Stand up and say something before you ruin this.

"Why did you stop?" she asked softly.

"I didn't want to stop." Mouth twitching, he glanced down at the hard-on fighting to push its way through the towel wrapped around his waist. "I think that much is obvious."

Peyton looked down, a smile curving up the corners of her lips, but only for the barest fraction of a second. Then she was frowning, looking more confused than ever.

"Then why did you?" she asked

It was impossible to miss the hurt and uncertainty there in her voice so he stepped closer, resting his hands on her hips. He hated the very thought that he could ever cause her even a second of pain.

"Because I'd like to take this slowly," he said.

She seemed even more confused than before by that declaration. Probably because guys weren't supposed to worry about stuff like that. They were supposed to worry about getting down to it. Right?

"My gut is telling me that we could have something amazing if we took the time to let it happen at its own pace," he said. "So, while I love kissing you, I'm willing to back off a bit to see what else we could be—besides naked."

Peyton gazed up at him for a long time and he was sure she was about to smack him...or call him crazy. Or both maybe. But then she smiled.

"I guess I can be patient for something amazing," she said.

Picking up her mug, she turned to walk out of the kitchen only to stop and look at him over her shoulder.

"But don't make me wait too long, okay?"

The words were a sultry whisper that raced straight from his ears to his cock and he had to reach for the towel to keep it around his hips as his hard-on did its best to fight its way free. And he was pretty sure Peyton saw it all before she disappeared from view.

Sighing, Noah picked up his cocoa, taking a long gulp of the hot liquid. SEAL training might have taught him how to deal with nearly every situation under the sun, but not this one. And when it came to Peyton, he was clearly in over his head.

Glancing down at the towel wrapped around his waist and the tent still being pitched there by his hard-on, he let out a snort.

"Come on, dumbass, let's get you back in the shower. It's obvious I won't be getting any sleep with you around and I don't see you going anywhere without a whole hell of a lot of cold water."

CHAPTER Seven

NOAH RESTED HIS HAND ON PEYTON'S LOWER BACK AS they walked toward the restaurant. She was so excited she was nearly skipping across the parking lot in her wedge heels and little black dress. While Noah had never said the word *date* this morning when he mentioned the SEAL promotion party tonight, as far as she was concerned, that's exactly what it was. A date with her bodyguard-turned-maybe something more.

Maybe something amazing.

Last night had been like something out of a fairytale. She'd come downstairs to tell him again how much she'd enjoyed dinner at his mom's place. She'd eaten there lots of times before and it had always been fun but being there with Noah made it even more special and she'd wanted him to know that. Then he'd stepped out of the bathroom wearing nothing but a towel and every thought in her head simply disappeared. Truthfully, Peyton couldn't even remember how they'd started kissing. She just remembered liking it.

When he'd pulled away, it had nearly crushed her. She'd been so sure he was rejecting her. It shouldn't have hurt one way or the other, but it had. More than she ever would have imagined. Then he told her why he'd hesitated, and it had been the sweetest, most romantic thing she'd ever heard. And for a woman who made a living writing romance, that was saying something.

She'd been so giddy afterward that it had taken forever to get to sleep. Instead, she'd laid in bed staring at the ceiling, trying to wrap her head around the idea that she and Noah could have something meaningful. A possibility made more amazing by the fact that a relationship with him wasn't something she'd even known she wanted. Especially since she'd kept telling herself they were too different. But when he suggested they could be amazing, she knew it was something she wanted with all of her heart. And she wanted it immediately.

The noise from the crowded restaurant hit

her all at once the moment Noah opened the door for her, and Peyton found herself questioning the idea of having a private party at a place this crowded.

"Don't worry," he said as he gave his name to the hostess standing at the front desk. "Sam and Nash reserved a private room in the back."

Peyton nodded as they followed the hostess through the restaurant with its huge central bar and dozens of TV's showing sporting events.

"So, Sam and Nash paid for all of this?" she asked, wanting to make sure she'd gotten that right. "I thought this was their promotion party. If that's the case, why do they have to pay?"

"It's a military tradition," Noah explained as the hostess pointed out a wide archway in the back of the restaurant, telling them their group was at the end of the hallway. "When a sailor gets promoted, they always pony up the pay increase from their first month's paycheck and throw a party for their Teammates. In this case, Sam and Nash pooled their money and paid for a private room and an hour's worth of free booze, which is also part of the tradition."

"They get promoted and have to pay for their own party?" she repeated, still not understanding.

"It seems like a crappy tradition to me. Shouldn't the person getting promoted be the one getting the free booze?"

"You'd think so." He chuckled. "But this particular tradition is less about celebrating another sailor's good fortune and more about using their newfound money to get drunk."

Peyton was about to point out how crazy that was when they walked into a big room filled with half a dozen banquet tables and the small bar that Noah had mentioned set up at the far end of the room. There was already about twenty people and her stomach tensed a little when she realized she didn't know any of them.

At Noah's prodding, Peyton had invited Laurissa to the party, but her friend wasn't there yet. Heck, she might not even come at all. Why would she want to hang out with her brother's Teammates anyway?

It was crazy to think that a group this size would bother her when she'd been in front of crowds of thousands. But those people had been there to meet Peyton Matthews, the writer, not Peyton Matthews, the girl going on a sort-of date with a Navy SEAL. Those were two different people.

"It's okay," Noah leaned in and whispered as if reading her mind. "This is simply a group of friends getting together for a night out. I promise, everyone is going to love you."

Peyton took a deep breath and steeled herself as some of his Teammates came over to give Noah a bro-hug and meet her.

"How's the knee doing?" Wes asked after most everyone else had drifted away, leaving her and Noah with Wes, his girlfriend, Kyla Wells, and their Teammate, Sam. "No more setbacks while working as Peyton's bodyguard?"

Noah jerked his head around, obviously checking to make sure no one outside their little circle had overheard. "Want to say that last part a little louder? I don't think they heard you in Cleveland."

Noah had warned her before coming to the party that they'd have to hide the whole bodyguard thing. Apparently, his boss thought he was spending his medical leave sitting on his couch playing video games. Noah had gone out of his way to make sure she understood how much trouble he'd be in if they found out he'd taken on outside employment. Peyton had promised not to say anything.

While Peyton chatted with Kyla, bonding over the fact that both of them had gone to San Diego State, she also listened in on the conversation Noah was having with Wes and Sam. A lot of it seemed to revolve around his injured knee, and from the way they were talking about it, she couldn't help but think there was more going on than he'd told her.

Peyton remembered Laurissa saying something about her brother hurting himself playing volleyball, but she swore she heard Sam say something about him getting injured *while over there.* She'd watched Noah do some exercises earlier this morning in her workout room and seen him grimace in pain when he put too much pressure on it in the wrong direction. There was no doubt in her mind it was probably more serious than he let on.

She didn't have a clue what SEALs did, but it wouldn't be shocking to imagine he'd hurt himself on a mission. It was a little disconcerting to think of him lying to his sister about it. Would he lie to her if she asked him for the truth?

Peyton was wondering about whether she wanted to know the answer to that question when another tall, muscular man approached them with a smile on his face, a woman with long, blond hair at his side. Peyton couldn't miss the way Noah's shoulders tensed, making her wonder who the guy was.

"Noah, glad you came," the man said, reaching out to shake hands while doing that shoulder-grippy thing guys did all the time.

"Wouldn't miss it," Noah said with a laugh, slipping his arm around her. "This is Peyton Matthews. Peyton, this is Chasen Ward my platoon's Chief Petty Officer and his wife, Hayley."

Peyton shook hands with the couple, smiling as Hayley hugged Noah, Wes, Kyla, and Sam. She once again got the sense that his Team was more like a family. It was nice.

A few moments later, Noah slipped away to get them drinks from the bar—since Sam and Nash were nice enough to pay for it—leaving her there alone with his friends.

"So, you're a full-time writer?" Chasen asked. "Is there good money in that?"

That earned him a smack on the arm from his wife, along with an eye roll. "Honey!"

"What?" he said. "It's a valid question. I like collecting information in case I decide to make a career change when I retire from the SEALs."

Peyton laughed. "I do okay." Like most writers, she didn't like talking about money. "But if you're serious about that second career thing, you might want to look elsewhere. The world of fiction publishing can be vicious."

"Oh, well," Hayley said with a sigh. "Guess you'll need to look elsewhere for your shot at fortune and fame."

Everyone was still laughing at that when Noah came back with her glass of white wine for her and a Jack and Coke for himself. It may have been her writer's imagination, but the drink seemed to fit him.

"Considering that I've never seen Noah read a book, how'd the two of you meet?" Chasen asked.

Peyton didn't say anything. She knew they couldn't reveal that Noah was her bodyguard, so she had no idea how to explain their meeting without revealing that particular detail, other than to say she knew his sister. She glanced out the corner of her eye, trying to let Noah know this one was completely on him.

"Actually, my sister introduced us," he said, flashing Peyton a grin and making it impossible to not smile back.

Chasen regarded Noah for a long moment,

but didn't say anything. Did he know Noah was hiding something?

Hayley was asking if Peyton lived in San Diego when she heard a familiar voice. She glanced over to see Laurissa coming toward them.

"You came!" Peyton said with a laugh as her friend ran over to hug her, interrupting the conversation she'd been having with Hayley. "I was worried you wouldn't be able make it with the short notice and everything."

Laurissa casually punched her much taller brother in the shoulder. "What, and leave you alone to deal with all this testosterone on your own? No chance!"

After Hayley and Chasen left to talk to some of the other people, the conversation quickly moved away from Noah and his ability to hide a secret, focusing on Sam's promotion and what he was going to do with all that extra money.

"Our pay doesn't really go up much," Sam said. "It's less than two hundred dollars a month after taxes. But the housing allowance goes up almost three hundred dollars a month, meaning I might actually be able to find a place I can afford off base and finally get out of the barracks."

Laurissa was asking Sam what kind of place

he was looking for when yet another tall, muscular man approached their group. Peyton did a double take. Did the Navy have some kind of cloning thing going on? Because like Noah, every man at the party was a physical specimen of perfection.

"You going to make introductions, dude, or you going to make me do it myself?" the man asked, looking back and forth between Peyton and Noah.

Noah snorted. "Peyton, this is Lane Robbins, a new member of our platoon and one of your more rabid fans."

Peyton laughed. She knew a super fan when she saw one and she was right, because Lane immediately began asking detailed questions about several obscure easter eggs he'd noticed in the most recent book. He'd even picked up on the scholarship letter the hero had received mid-book without fan fair of any type. They were talking about the book signing she'd be doing the next day and whether Lane would be able to make it when Noah interrupted.

"Sorry to break this up, but before she punches me in the arm again for not introducing her, Lane, this is my sister, Laurissa. And before you ask, no, she's not available."

It was Peyton's turn to let out a snort at the blatant way Noah declared his sister off limits, something which earned him that aforementioned punch in the arm he'd been trying to avoid. After giving Noah a glare, Laurissa smiled at Lane and held out her hand.

"I know you from somewhere, don't I?" Laurissa asked, gazing up at Lane curiously for a moment before her eyes went wide. "Wait a minute! You're on my to-do list."

Noah frowned, clearly not liking the sound of that. "What's a *to-do list* and why do you have one?"

Most of the people in the room were looking in their direction now, and all of them seemed just as amused as Peyton by the whole exchange.

"That's what I call the people I consider serious contenders on Tinder that I haven't gotten around to messaging yet," Laurissa said, giving him a sweet smile. "In fact, now that I think about it, Lane is at the top of the list."

While that clearly pleased Lane if the broad grin on his face was anything to go by, poor Noah, on the other hand, looked like he was about to blow a gasket. As for his Teammates, they seemed to think this was the best thing ever.

"Does Mom know you're fishing for hook-ups on a dating app?" Noah whispered urgently, as if the rest of the room couldn't hear him. "She's going to lose her mind when she finds out."

Laurissa laughed. "Who do you think helped me set up my profile?"

"Please tell me you're joking," Noah begged, and Peyton thought for a minute he might pass out.

His sister made a face. "Of course, I'm joking. I don't even think Mom knows what Tinder is."

Peyton hid her smile in her glass as she took a sip of wine. While Noah appeared to be relieved at that, he still didn't seem to like the idea of Laurissa and Lane together. Before he could say anything else, two servers came in and announced they were ready to start taking orders for dinner. Laurissa took that as the signal to go find a seat at one of the tables—with Lane. Noah was about to follow, but Peyton caught his hand, leading him to a different one.

He glared at Lane, who blatantly ignored him. "I don't think I want my sister seeing someone on my Team."

"And I don't think Laurissa cares what you think," Peyton pointed out as they sat down. "So, maybe let your sister handle her own dating life while we focus on dinner?"

She expected some resistance to that suggestion, but after a moment, Noah sighed and nodded, giving her his full attention and asking if she'd ever eaten at the restaurant before.

The next two hours turned into the best date Peyton had been on in a long time. She spent some of the time chatting with Kyla and Wes, who sat near them, but mostly she and Noah focused on each other as if they were the only ones in the room.

She wasn't sure what they even talked about. Just...stuff. TV shows and movies they'd seen, their favorite family pets growing up, their love of scuba diving and dislike for broccoli. She even confessed she preferred swimming in the ocean to lying on the beach.

"There are simply so many places sand was never meant to be," she told him with a laugh.

After the promotion party officially ended, Sam and Nash dragged everyone to the bar in the main restaurant for another round of free drinks. Their huge group crowded into the small area, the guys immediately getting the bartender's attention.

Peyton gave Laurissa a grin. "So, you and Lane, huh?"

Laurissa laughed, glancing at the cute SEAL standing over by the bar. "I'd been planning to try and set up a date with Lane even before meeting him tonight. But now that we have, there's no doubt in my mind we'd be a good fit. He's even more handsome in person than in his picture—and I thought he was hot then. He's so easy to talk to. And it's definitely a bonus that Noah doesn't like the idea of me dating Lane. I live to make him uncomfortable."

"That's so wrong," Peyton said, shaking her head but laughing all the same. "He's your brother. You should be nicer to him."

Laurissa lifted a brow. "Defending my brother now, huh? And before you try and deny it, don't think I didn't notice how into each other the two of you were at dinner. When did Noah go from being your bodyguard to something more?"

Peyton opened her mouth to say there was nothing going on, but then closed it again. Laurissa was her best friend in the world. She couldn't lie to her.

"We kissed last night," she admitted softly. "And it was really good. Better than good. The most amazing kiss ever. I was ready to go so much further, but Noah wanted to slow down because he thought there could be something special happening between us. So, we're going to take our time and see where things take us. I guess tonight was technically our first date. Is that okay? Me dating your brother, I mean. That won't make it weird for you, will it?"

"Why would it make it weird?" Laurissa smiled. "My two favorite people in the world are getting together. What could be better than that? You've always been like a sister to me, so being my sister-in-law would be awesome."

Peyton laughed. "While it's a relief you feel that way, I think it's safe to say you can put the brakes on when it comes to that sister-in-law stuff. Like I said, this was technically only our first date."

"Who are you kidding?" Laurissa let out a snort. "You guys could have been alone in that room back there for all the attention you paid anyone else. It's obvious you two are perfect for each other."

Peyton was about to thank her friend for the vote of confidence, but the serious expression that suddenly crossed Laurissa's face stopped her.

"What is it?" she asked.

Laurissa hesitated, like she was wondering if she should say anything, then sighed. "I don't want this to sound like I'm trying to say you *shouldn't* be with Noah, but have you thought about what dating a SEAL is going to be like? I mean, it's not like I keep track of what he's doing on a day-to-day basis, but I know he's gone a lot. Even worse, he can't tell us anything about where he's going or what he's doing. Most of the time we don't even know he left town until he misses a dinner at Mom's house or a movie with me."

Peyton considered that. She'd been so focused on the idea of spending time with a man as perfect as Noah that the reality of his job had almost been an afterthought.

"I don't know a lot about what SEALs do," she admitted. "All I know is what I've read in a handful of military romances and what I see on the news. I'd like to think he's well trained, good at his job, and that his Teammates watch out for him."

"I'm sure you're right about all those things, but bad things can still happen." Her brow creased. "Regardless of what he says, I'm almost certain he didn't hurt his knee playing volleyball. He was almost assuredly on a mission, probably in some backwater craphole neither one of us could find on a map if our lives depended on it."

When Peyton didn't say anything, her friend leaned in and gave her a hug, then stepped back to look at her seriously. "I would never try and tell you not to date my brother. You're a grown woman free to make your own choices. I only want you to think about what it will mean if you do and ask yourself if you're ready for what being with a Navy SEAL means."

CHAPTER

PEYTON GROANED, BLINKING AT THE EARLY MORNING sun streaming through her bedroom window. *Crap.* She felt like she hadn't slept at all last night. That wasn't surprising considering the questions Laurissa had given her to ponder at the promotion party.

She doubted her friend had intended for her to lose sleep over any of it, but that was one of Peyton's many failings. If there was a problem, she nonstop obsessed about it until it was solved. Unfortunately, in this case, there was no simple solution. Which was why she'd spent hours staring up at the ceiling last night wondering if she was making a big mistake falling for Noah.

Part of her knew she was blowing the whole thing out of proportion. She'd known Noah for all of seventy-two hours and they'd gone on exactly one unofficial date. Yet here she was, getting wrapped around the axle worrying about whether she could handle him being a SEAL. Then again, that was standard practice for her. She had a history of worrying about the long-term potential of a relationship before the first date was even in the books.

She didn't know what that said about her. She'd simply never had the slightest interest in having a casual thing with a guy. Unlike Laurissa, she wasn't the swipe-right kind of girl. Heck, she'd never even dated more than one guy at a time. If she went out with someone, she committed to him until they went their separate ways.

Maybe that was why Laurissa told her to think long and hard about whether she wanted to get involved with Noah. Maybe she knew they'd never work out.

Rolling onto her back, Peyton dragged the pillow over her face to scream into it. Leave it to her to find a whole new way to torture herself.

Get a grip.

Sighing, she sat up and swung her legs over the side of the bed. This situation wasn't nearly as complicated as she was making it out to be.

On one hand, she liked Noah. A lot. Enough

to already see herself in a relationship with him, regardless of the fact that she'd only known him for three days. On the other, Noah had a job that would scare off most sane women. Was she going to let his job scare her off, too?

Her first instinct was to say, hell no. But then she took a breath and stopped herself. If she was being honest, Laurissa's warning that Noah was gone all the time on secret missions that nobody even knew about was enough to give her pause.

How could she live not knowing if he was safe or not?

How could *any* woman live like that?

Getting to her feet, Peyton took off her tank top and shorts and put on her yoga clothes.

Obviously, there were women who did live like that. Hayley and Chasen had recently gotten married. Kyla and Wes seemed to be headed that way. And there had been other women at the party last night who'd appeared equally committed to the SEALs they were dating, some married and others engaged. They weren't superhuman. They were simply in love. If other women could do it, she had to believe she could, too.

But before she could know for sure, she'd need more than a vague idea of what Noah and his fellow SEALs did for a living. She also needed to know exactly what he wanted out of this relationship. He'd said he wanted to see what else they could be. Was his idea of a future for them the same as hers?

Peyton decided to do without her usual bottle of water, not needing the distraction of a half-naked Noah sleeping on her couch, and went directly to her workout room. After the night she had, skipping yoga wasn't an option. Thirty minutes of chaturangas, downward dog, and warrior positions would not only refresh her, but get her completely ready for the party later that would include a couple hundred die-hard fans and one very distracting SEAL.

After a quick workout and a shower, Peyton changed into a skirt and sleeveless top, then headed downstairs. Noah was leaning back against the counter in the kitchen, scrolling through his phone with one hand and holding a mug of coffee in the other. He glanced up as she walked in, his eyes lingering on her for a moment before he went back to his phone. Peyton smiled to herself, enjoying the sensation of his warm gaze on her skin.

"Morning," he said, looking up from the

phone again with an expression that could only be described as hungry. She found herself relishing that thought.

"Good morning," she replied, taking out a mug and filling it with coffee. "Have you eaten yet?"

He shook his head. "I waited for you."

That was nice of him. And exactly what a guy who was into her would do.

Peyton got two bowls out of the cabinet, then took a detour to the pantry for the cereal. When she came back out, Noah already had the carton of coconut-almond milk on the table and two spoons. She handed him one of the bowls, then sat down opposite him. As tempting as it was to gaze at him the whole time they ate, she limited herself to quick glances.

"Okay, tell me about this book signing/release party thing we're doing tonight," he said.

"There's not much to tell," she said, filling her bowl with Cheerios, then adding milk. "My publisher has reserved a large ballroom at the Hilton San Diego Bayfront and the event is supposed to kick off at six PM, though they rarely get these things off exactly on time. I usually go into the ballroom through a side entrance after all the fans have arrived and been given instructions on how the book signing will work. Then I stand at a podium and say a few words to welcome my readers and talk about the series and the newest book, tease a few tidbits about what comes next, answer a few questions from fans. After that, I spend the next four hours signing books. I know it sounds a little chaotic, but it's actually rather chill and routine when you get right down to it."

Noah seemed to consider that for a while, and from his slightly distracted expression, she got the feeling he was probably going through various security issues with the event she just described.

"Are the people who put this event together aware of the threat against you?" he asked. "Have they given any thought to postponing it or holding it in a more secure location?"

"The only person who knows about the break-in is my senior editor, Gwen Williamson." She dipped her spoon into her cereal. "My publisher has decided to keep everyone else in the dark. Less chance it will leak to the press that way. And as far as postponing the event or moving it somewhere? No chance. This thing has been planned for months and coincided with the official release of the book next week. The release date can't be changed at this point and with many of my readers coming from out of town just for a chance to meet me, there's no way we can move the party. It would be a public relations catastrophe. Even if we could, I wouldn't treat my readers like that. It's wrong."

On the other side of the table, Noah scowled, but didn't say anything.

"I know you're worried about me and I appreciate that more than you'll ever know," she said. "But I can't live like a shut-in until this book is finished. I have obligations to my publisher beyond writing, not the least of which is this release party. Over the next few weeks, I'll have quite a few signings at bookstores around town and a few interviews, too."

"I know." He filled his own bowl with cereal and began to eat it—dry. "But I still worry about having you out in public like this. And yeah, I know we went out last night, but that was completely different. Nobody knew you were going to be there. Like you said, this release party has been publicized for months. If someone wanted to get to you outside of your home, that would be the place to do it."

"Maybe," she agreed, more than a little nervous

at the thought. "But I trust you to keep me safe. I know you won't let me out of your sight."

While they ate, they talked a little more about the other book signings and interviews she'd be doing. After they were finished Peyton rinsed their bowls before putting them in the washer.

"I'm going to head back upstairs and get a couple hours of writing done before we leave," she said.

He frowned. "A couple hours? I thought you said the release party isn't until six. We don't need to leave for like eight hours or something."

"If we were heading straight to the Bayfront hotel, yes," she told him. "But I need to get my hair and nails done before the party and my appointment at the salon is at two o'clock. And since this is a dressy event, we'll need to get you something else to wear besides jeans."

"You mean, like a suit?"

She nodded, then almost laughed as his mouth twitched in the cutest way she'd ever seen.

"We'll have to stop by my place so I can pick it up then," he said.

That worked for her. And considering how good he looked in everything from jeans and a T-shirt to a towel, she couldn't wait to see him dressed up.

"I have to admit, your place is a lot neater than I expected," Peyton said as they walked into his apartment. "I don't know why, I assumed it would be your standard bachelor pad with dishes piled up in the sink and pizza boxes overflowing the garbage can." She gave him an apologetic look. "Does that make me a bad person?"

Noah chuckled, catching a whiff of the shampoo they used at the salon and he couldn't help inhaling appreciatively. He still wasn't sure what a blow-out was, but the two-plus hours he'd waited for her at the salon was definitely worth it. She looked amazing.

"Considering I told you I could eat pizza every night of the week, no, it doesn't," he said. "When you go on missions with no notice, you keep your place as clean as you can."

He didn't mention that before he'd left for her place the other day, he had to toss out an entire trash bag full of burger wrappers, pizza boxes, and chip bags that had accumulated while he'd been on medical leave.

Closing the door, he pocketed his keys. “I learned the hard way that there’s nothing worse than coming home to a sink full of dirty dishes after a month-long deployment. It helps that the place is so small. It makes it easy to keep up with it.”

“I don’t know,” Peyton said, glancing around. “It’s a pretty roomy apartment for a single guy. And that deck is like having an extra living room.”

While nowhere near as big as her house on the beach, Noah supposed he couldn’t really complain. His second-floor apartment had a fancy kitchen, two bedrooms, one-and-a-half baths, and an outdoor grill that was the envy of the neighbors.

Noah was mesmerized for a moment, watching Peyton gaze at the framed photos mounted on the walls, and the trinkets and knickknacks from his travels set out here and there. He realized he liked her in his space. She looked good here.

“I’m going to grab my suit,” he forced himself to say, finally remembering why they were there in the first place. “Make yourself at home.”

Peyton nodded, her attention focused on the photos.

Noah walked into his bedroom and over to

the closet. As he flipped through the mix of military and civilian clothes, he replayed the past few hours. He'd never been to a salon before, and after the one he'd gone to with Peyton, he doubted he ever would. It'd definitely been one of the stranger experiences of his life.

It had been one of those fancy places with lots of potted plants, scented candles, and a waterfall feature right in the middle of the waiting area. In the background, a soundtrack of tranquil music and rain forest sounds had been playing. He supposed it was meant to be relaxing, but it made him feel like he'd been trapped in an elevator.

Peyton had told him she'd be a while, suggesting he might want to head out and find a bookstore or some other place to wait until she was done. But there was no way he was going to leave her unguarded, so he'd settled in one of the stuffed chairs in the lobby to wait.

They didn't have any magazines he could see himself reading—women's fashion wasn't his thing—but after spending an hour reading the latest college football preseason news on his phone, he'd been desperate enough to try anything and finally picked up a copy of *Cosmo*. If he'd gotten strange looks from the salon's clients before, that was nothing compared to how they'd eyed him when they saw him flipping through an article on the wildest sex positions ever published. Truthfully, they didn't seem that wild to him. Some even looked sort of boring. And quite a few of the rest were likely physically impossible unless you were made out of rubber.

But as strange as it was to be sitting in a salon reading a *Cosmo*, the thing that weirded him out the most was all the women who kept asking if he'd like to get his hair done while he waited. When he politely declined—several times—they decided to offer him a mani-pedi.

"All the men are getting them now," a freckled redhead had told him, staring at his hands with an intensity that actually scared him a little.

Noah could comfortably say he'd never met a man who'd gotten a mani-pedi. And he could also comfortably say he'd lived for twenty-eight years without getting his nails filed and buffed and that he was pretty sure he didn't need to start now. Trying to convince the women who worked at the salon of that fact was harder than he thought it'd be. They were scary aggressive when it came to talking up their services. Kind of like the people who tried to sell you timeshare rentals at the beach.

He'd never been so relieved when Peyton had finally come out and rescued him. He'd been so rattled he'd barely remembered to tell her how beautiful she looked.

Shaking his head at the memory, Noah found his favorite dark charcoal suit to one side of his closet and pulled it out. Thankfully, the Team commander had talked him into getting it a while ago. Up until that point, Noah had worn his Navy whites to formal functions. It'd seemed like a waste of money to splurge on a suit, but he had to admit it was the best money he ever spent.

If nothing else, the suit was proving to be a lifesaver for Peyton's big release party. Without it, he would have been forced to go on a shopping spree with her. And while he enjoyed hanging out with her, shopping was not how he preferred to spend that time.

He stuffed the suit in a nylon garment bag, then added a light-blue dress shirt before tossing a tie in a small overnight bag along with a pair of socks and black dress shoes. Doing a quick mental inventory to make sure he hadn't forgotten anything, he zipped the bags, then turned for the door and stopped, his gaze locking on the gun safe in the back of the closest. He paused for a moment, wondering if he should take a weapon with him tonight. He had a small frame 9mm automatic it there, along with a slimline holster designed to fit inside the waist of his suit pants. No one would even see it.

Unless he had to pull it out of course.

Then someone would certainly see it and he'd be screwed. Yes, it would add an extra level of protection if something happened, but at the same time, if he drew a weapon that he had no concealed carry permit for, he'd end up in jail. And likely in trouble with Chasen and headquarters.

After hesitating for a few more seconds, Noah shook his head, then headed back into the living room. He only hoped he didn't regret this decision.

Peyton was standing by the fireplace looking at the framed photos on the mantel and those along the wall. There were some of him with his mom and sister, but most were of him with his SEAL Team or places he'd gotten to visit. Noah set down the overnight bag, then draped the garment one over the back of the couch and walked over to stand beside her.

She glanced at him, her lips curving into a smile. "I recognize a lot of these guys from the promotion party the other night, but not all of them."

He motioned at one of the group photos. "These four are on a mission overseas. And these three were all medically discharged from the SEALs due to injuries sustained in the line of duty."

Her gaze lingered on a photo of him and the other guys with a dilapidated-looking mud hut in the background. "Do you still stay in touch with the guys who got discharged from the Navy?"

He grinned. "For sure. Those guys are like my brothers. There's nothing I wouldn't do for them and vice versa. If any of them called and said he needed me to go halfway across the world to help him, I'd go without hesitation."

Peyton turned to face him, her expression tough to read as she looked up at him. "Having a bond like that sounds amazing."

They hadn't been this close to each other since the party last night and her nearness was making it hard to think of anything except kissing her again. "Um, yeah."

Way to sound articulate, dude.

"What about this guy on the end?" she asked, smiling as if she knew he was a little befuddled. "I'm pretty sure I didn't see him at the party, either."

Noah didn't say anything for a second, not sure how he was supposed to answer the question, since Peyton wasn't going to like hearing the truth. "That's Dan," he said softly, reaching out to run a finger over the frame. "He died on a mission about a year ago. We were good friends."

Seeing Peyton's eyes fill with sadness made him sorry he'd told her. Maybe a lie would have been better. But then he realized that would have been stupid. He'd spent a good portion of the past few days wondering if he and Peyton might be right for each other. If she couldn't handle the simple reality of life in the SEALs, then getting together with her was nothing but a pipe dream.

"Oh. I'm so sorry," she murmured. "How did it happen? Did they get the people who did it? I mean, they didn't get away with it, did they?"

They were typical questions people asked when they heard that anyone in the military had died in combat, so he didn't blame her for wondering.

"There's not much I can tell you," he said. "It

was a classified operation, so the location and details were never released."

Peyton didn't say anything for a long time, turning to look at the photos on the mantle and wall again, only to settle on Dan's picture. Noah was about to apologize for saying something so disturbing when she spoke.

"I guess that's what Laurissa meant when she asked me if I'd really thought about what it would be like to get involved with a SEAL."

Noah opened his mouth, wanting to know exactly what his sister had said, but Peyton turned back then, her expression serious.

"It's not like she was trying to warn me off," she said. "I want you to know that. But she told me in the strongest terms possible that you travel all the time, that you can't tell anyone where you're going or when you'll get back, and that sometimes bad things happen. I told myself I understood all that, but after telling me about Dan, I'm not so sure I was being honest with myself."

Part of him was pissed Laurissa had inserted herself into the middle of this, but another part realized he couldn't hold it against his sister for looking out for him...and for Peyton.

"When did you two talk about this?" he asked.

"The party," Peyton said. "She picked up on the vibe between us during dinner and asked me when things changed between us. I told her about the kiss and that we were going to take it slow. She was thrilled for us, but also concerned I was going into this with my eyes not quite wide open."

Noah took a deep breath, letting it out in a sigh. Putting his hands on her waist, he gently tugged her closer and gazed deep into her eyes. He had this conversation with other women before. Not usually this soon, but it happened every time and it never got easier. But for some reason, it seemed even harder this time. Because he didn't want to watch Peyton walk away.

"I wish I could say my sister was wrong, but she isn't," he said slowly, bring her in until his chin was resting on the top of her head and her face was buried against his chest. "I'm a SEAL. That means the phone will sometimes ring in the middle of the night and I'll have to go. I might be gone for a week or six months, and I won't be able to tell you anything one way or the other. I'm always careful, but what I do *is* dangerous. There's no way to hide from that."

She didn't say anything. Knowing that wasn't

a good sign, he kept going, hoping this time things might turn out differently.

"The last thing I want to do is scare you off, but at the same time, I also don't want you getting hurt when you realize being with me is more than you signed up for. I don't ever want to hurt you."

Peyton nodded against his chest. A moment later, she took a step back and reached a hand up to quickly wipe a tear from her cheek.

"We should probably get going if we're going to make it to the release party on time," she said softly. "We have to get back home in time for me to change, and should probably get something to eat, too. Once the signing starts, I'm not going to be able to take a break for anything more than a sip of water."

Her voice was casual, but there was a sadness in her eyes that made Noah think he'd destroyed any shot he ever had with this amazing woman. All because he'd decided to be honest and upfront about everything.

Sometimes, he could be such a dumbass.

CHAPTER

THEY STOPPED AT P.F. CHANG'S FOR TAKEOUT ON THE way back to Peyton's house. Neither of them said a word throughout the drive or the stop at the restaurant. Was this what it would be like for the rest of the time he was guarding her?

But the mood changed drastically once they got home and spread the containers of spicy chicken and brown rice around the kitchen table. It was almost like Peyton had let go of whatever emotion had taken hold of her after the discussion at his place. By the time they sat down to eat, that sense of intimacy they'd shared before returned, and Noah almost convinced himself the distance he'd felt between them during the drive home had been his imagination.

While she got dressed for the party, Noah sent a quick group text to Wes, Sam, and Lane, asking if any of them were available for backup at the release party. All three of his buddies replied right away, saying they'd be there.

He took a quick shower in the downstairs bathroom then put on his suit. He was tying his tie in front of the mirror above the vanity when he heard Peyton's high heels echo on the wood floor in the living room. He walked out to meet her and almost fell over his own feet at the sight of her standing there.

The blue gown she wore didn't show any cleavage or have a slit that showed a flash of leg, or anything remotely like that. Yet Noah had never seen a woman look sexier in his life. He couldn't take his eyes off her.

"You look gorgeous," he said.

She looked him up and down, her lips curving into a smile. "You clean up pretty nice yourself."

If he didn't know better, he'd think she was mentally undressing him right now. That was an image he didn't need. Not if he had any hope of keeping his mind focused on keeping her safe tonight.

Noah tore his gaze away from her and slipped into his suit jacket, then grabbed his keys, phone, and wallet off the coffee table, shoving the latter into his back pocket.

"Ready to go?" he asked.

She nodded. "I am if you are."

As they walked out to his SUV, Noah couldn't help thinking this felt a lot like a date. No doubt that would change when they got to the release party and there were hundreds of fans screaming Peyton's name.

"So, what are one of these release parties like?" he asked as he turned onto the street outside her home and headed for the bay.

"Fun, crazy, and exhausting all at the same time."

"That doesn't tell me much," he said drily. "I was more interested in the tactical details. Things that are critical to your safety."

She laughed. "I wouldn't know a tactical detail if I fell over it. What exactly do you want to know?"

"For starters, how many people will probably be there?"

She thought a moment, starting to count on her fingers. "Well, counting my publisher, editor, assistant editors, publicity people, Laurissa, and Tabitha...maybe five or six hundred."

He did a double take so fast the SUV swerved a little. "Are you serious?"

"Uh-huh." Peyton flashed him a smile. "Don't look so alarmed. Since most of my readers tend to be under twenty-one, there won't be any alcohol served, so things won't get too wild. Unless we run out of books."

Noah had visions of readers trampling each other to get the last few books, like a crazy Black Friday sale, punches being thrown when they realized there weren't enough to go around.

"You're kidding, right?"

"Of course, I'm kidding. We won't run out of books. Even if we did, no one is going to get into a fight over it," she said. "My readers aren't like that. They're there to hang out and have a good time. Some of them even come dressed up as the characters from my books."

He gave her a sidelong glance. "Now you really are pulling my leg."

"I'm not," she insisted. "You can't spell fanatic without fan, you know?"

"That's crazy."

Peyton shrugged. "I think it's fun."

Noah turned onto the road leading to the hotel. "How close do fans usually get to you?"

"Close enough to take selfies, along with copious amounts of hugs, jumping up and down, and squealing."

He frowned. After seeing how Tabitha reacted to Peyton, he should have figured that. In his mind, that was a little too close for comfort.

Peyton put her hand on his arm. It felt nice. Especially after their earlier conversation and the way things had been left. "Stop worrying so much. I've done lots of these parties and nothing ever happened."

"Someone wasn't trying to steal your book then," he pointed out. "And where is your book? Still in your purse?"

She nodded, but her happy mood dimmed a bit at his reminder, and he cursed himself for being so damn practical all the time.

Noah saw the crowds before he even pulled into the hotel driveway, and that familiar tension he felt before going into combat began to fill his stomach.

"There's been no other attempt to steal the book since that first break-in, so you probably think that means you're no longer in danger." He weaved through the other cars toward the valet stand. "But the opposite is true. It means they know the book isn't in your house and that you keep it on you. This release party would be the easiest place to get to you. The fact that there are hundreds of people around to use as cover will only make it easier for whoever this person is."

He came to a stop in front of the valet stand, then put the SUV in park and turned to look at her. "If someone or something at the party looks suspicious, they probably are, so don't do anything foolish tonight. And don't put yourself in a situation where we get separated, okay?"

She gazed at him for a moment, then nodded. "Okay."

CHAPTER
Ten

PEYTON'S RED-HAIRED, FRECKLED PUBLICIST, CLAIRE Newton, met her and Noah at the front door and escorted them through the lobby toward the main ballroom. Noah was a reassuring presence behind them, but Peyton would have preferred him at her side so they could hold hands and enjoy the party with him as a boyfriend instead of a bodyguard. But they couldn't do that, especially after the conversation they had earlier at his apartment.

Moving through the crowd, waving hello to the fans who were still maintaining their distance at this point, Peyton found herself thinking about what he'd said...and how it had nearly crushed her heart.

She knew Noah hadn't meant to be hurtful. And he hadn't said anything she didn't already know. But there was a drastic difference between understanding that being a SEAL was dangerous and looking at photos of a real person who'd paid the price for doing the job. The calm way Noah talked about friends who'd been injured and those who'd been killed had rattled her so badly she hadn't been able to think much less talk until they got back to her place.

She was sure Noah had taken her stunned silence as confirmation that she wasn't ready to live in his world and while that wasn't necessarily true, she didn't know how to tell him how she really felt. Mostly because she wasn't sure. Maybe it was better to stop seeing him altogether after this bodyguard thing was over since it seemed like that's where this was all headed anyway.

Peyton was so wrapped up in that depressing thought she didn't realize they'd reached the green room until Laurissa and Tabitha were in front of her, smiling like crazy and going on and on about the number of fans waiting for her in the main ballroom. That was when she noticed other people in the small space, looking at her expectantly.

Crap. She needed to get it together.

Hugging Laurissa and Tabitha, she then did

the same to her editor, Gwen Williamson, asking how her flight from New York was. Tall and reed thin with blond hair, Gwen hugged her back, murmuring something about turbulence over the Midwest, before stepping back to let Peyton greet her assistant editors, Hannah Anderson and Scott Moore. Hannah was right out of college and still learning the business, while Scott was an old hand who'd been with Peyton from the very beginning. Lately, Scott had been less involved in her series because he was busy taking on new writers. She hated not working with Scott as much, but that was the way it worked in publishing. Besides, it was definitely time for him to take on new authors of his own.

As Claire ducked out to check on something for the party, Peyton introduced Noah to everyone, saying he was a friend. No one except Gwen knew he was her bodyguard and she intended to keep it that way.

"He's never been to one of these things and I thought he'd enjoy a look behind the scenes," she added.

She was going over the evening's schedule with Laurissa and Tabitha when Kiki Rowe, the artist who did the covers for her books, walked in.

Instead of running over and hugging Peyton like she usually did, Kiki stopped and stared at Noah. It was difficult not to. He was standing there looking like the best dressed Adonis that ever existed.

"I don't know who you are, but have you ever considered doing any modeling?" Kiki studied Noah, looking at his face from all angles, like she was imagining what she could do with him on a cover. "You're incredibly attractive, but still ruggedly masculine. I put you in a military uniform and the cover alone will sell a thousand copies before anyone bothers to see what the book is about."

Peyton almost burst out laughing at the startled expression that crossed Noah's face. She wasn't sure if he was offended at the idea of being looked at like a piece of meat or that he was only guaranteed to sell a thousand copies.

"I'm guessing that's the bodyguard Em hired to protect you?" Gwen said, gently moving Peyton to the side so they could talk privately while Noah fended off Kiki. "The one who insisted that give whatever we give whatever we pay him to a military charity? Where the heck did you find him, Chippendales?"

Peyton smiled. "Yes, he's the bodyguard. And

no, he's not a male stripper. He's an active-duty Navy SEAL who agreed to help because he's Laurissa's brother."

Gwen squinted at Noah over the top of her glasses, nodding her approval as if pleased with Peyton's choice of bodyguards. Then again, Gwen could simply be mentally undressing Noah. Even the extremely quiet Hannah had gone all dreamy-eyed.

The only one who didn't look impressed by Noah was Scott, and only because he was a straight guy. Instead, he stood there looking bored, twirling that pen he always carried between his fingers the whole time. She might love working with him, but crap, that was an annoying habit.

"The ballroom is packed and there are still more readers waiting to get in," Claire said, hurrying into the room with a grin. "I seriously think we might be in danger of actually running out of books this time. Do you need to run to the ladies' room or anything before going into the ballroom? You might not get another chance after everything starts."

Peyton smiled. "No, I'm good. Let's do this."

She glanced at Noah as they headed inside,

almost laughing. He looked like he was walking into enemy territory rather than a room full of what she knew for a fact were the best readers in the world. None of them would ever try to hurt her. She tried to convey that to him with a smile, but he was already surveying the room for potential threats.

Peyton sighed. If Noah had his way, he'd probably whisk her into the ballroom through a service entrance and keep everyone half the length of a football field away, only letting them approach to have a book signed. Even then, he'd likely want to keep them at arm's length. But she would miss out on interacting with her readers and that wouldn't be fair. She'd always been accessible to them and wasn't going to change now. Knowing Noah was concerned for her was endearing—even if it was his job—but she honestly didn't think there was any danger of the bad guy infiltrating the release party since most of the people attending were teenage girls.

Noah took up a position at the rear of the stage area, probably thinking he was being inconspicuous. That was crazy of course. There were a lot of women in the ballroom who'd caught sight of him and couldn't keep their eyes off him. She didn't blame them. If Noah wasn't standing behind her, she'd be staring at him, too.

She was almost at the end of the little speech Claire had helped her put together when she spotted Noah's Teammate, Sam, in the back of the ballroom. She almost stumbled over the story she was telling about meeting her very first fan, but recovered just in time to see Wes over by the archway that led to the kitchen. Noah must have asked his friends to provide some extra protection. It was almost certainly overkill, but very sweet nonetheless.

A second later she saw Lane, smiling broadly as he realized she'd noticed him. Either that or he was really psyched at being at the book signing. She'd have to remember to keep a book to the side. He deserved a signed copy for showing up here. Even if he was a closet superfan.

Noah stuck close when the signing started, and readers began jumping in to take group selfies with five or more people at a time. Peyton laughed, wishing he could let himself relax. But no. Instead, he looked poised to attack the entire four hours. She wasn't sure how he did it. Seriously, it seemed exhausting to her.

As the last few readers hurried over for one

more hug—and a few more easter eggs from the next book—Noah moved even closer. He looked ready to shove them out the door, but Peyton waved him off. She absolutely loved this part of her job and could do it all night.

"See?" she said as the remaining teenage girl paused on her way out of the ballroom to give Peyton a big wave. "I told you everything would be fine tonight."

Noah opened his mouth to answer, but before he could say anything, Gwen and Claire showed up with Heather, Kiki, and Scott, all of them talking excitedly about how fantastic the release party had gone.

"Did you have a good time, Noah?" Kiki asked, still looking at him like she was sizing him up for her next book cover. Or some indecent pics she could keep under her pillow. "And have you reconsidered the modeling career?"

"Yes and no," Noah said in a completely flat tone that pretty much ensured Kiki picked up on the fact that the small talk part of the evening was over.

Peyton bit her tongue to keep from laughing as Claire filled her in on the details of the next few promotional events. When her publicist was done, Gwen then asked about the status of her next book. It wasn't due for two weeks, but they always pushed her to turn manuscripts in early. Peyton got about four months to write it and the publisher got twice that to check for typos and point out problem areas. There was something inherently unequal in this division of labor agreement, at least from Peyton's perspective.

"I'm close to wrapping everything up," she assured her editors.

"Excellent!" Gwen said. "Why don't I stop by tomorrow and take a look at what you have so far. Just to give marketing something to work with. Get ahead of the game, you know?"

Yeah, Peyton did know. They wanted the book early and badgered her until they got it.

A few minutes later, Gwen and the rest of the crew left to grab a late-night snack at the hotel restaurant, leaving Peyton and Noah alone in the ballroom for all of two minutes before the hotel staff came in and started breaking down tables and dragging away the chairs.

Peyton was more than ready to head home. She might be riding the endorphin high of being around so many readers right now, but she'd crash at some point. But as she and Noah headed for the door, her three other bodyguards arrived, along with Laurissa and Tabitha, smiles on their faces.

"That was unreal," Lane said with a laugh. "I've never seen anything like that. There were so many people and they were all fans of your books!"

Peyton couldn't help laughing along with Lane, realizing that he'd been as caught up in the excitement as all her other readers had.

"Speaking of fans," she said, reaching into her big purse and coming out with the book she'd remembered to set aside. "This is for you."

Lane stared at the book for a second, then flipped open the front cover to look at the words she'd written inside. His smile widened. "This is awesome! Thanks!"

"The signing went smoother than I thought it would," Wes said, shaking his head as Lane immediately started flipping through the book. "When we first pulled up and saw all the people, I had visions of you being crushed as hundreds of people rushed the table to get their books signed. But this thing went off without a hitch."

Peyton would have chatted longer, but the hotel staff politely nudged them out of the room a few moments later so they could finish cleaning up.

"You guys feel like grabbing pizza with us?" Sam asked as they walked into the lobby. "I know this great place a few miles from here."

Noah threw Peyton a look before shaking his head. "Thanks for the offer, but I think we're going to head home. It's been a long night."

She sighed. "While I'd love to, Noah's right. Besides, I need to get a little writing done before bed."

They all seemed bummed she and Noah wouldn't be joining them, but said they understood. Before they took off, Sam asked if he and the other guys should hang around until the valet brought his vehicle, but Noah shook his head.

"We're good," he said. "If someone was planning to make a move against Peyton, it would have been during the signing when there were people everywhere."

After hugs all around, Sam and the other guys left with Laurissa and Tabitha.

"Did you have fun?" Noah asked, moving them past the people hanging around outside the hotel, including two guys arguing about their fantasy football stats.

"I did," Peyton said, liking the feel of Noah's hand on her lower back. It was warm and comforting. "I've loved doing book signings since the first one I went to years ago."

While they waited for the valet to bring Noah's SUV around, they talked about other book signings she'd done until they got interrupted by shouting from halfway down the sidewalk. It was those two guys and their fantasy football argument, which seemed to be getting heated.

"Wonder what their problem is?" she said.

"I don't know, but they both sound like they're pissed and drunk as hell," Noah muttered. "Those kinds of things usually never end well."

"You sound like you speak from experience."

He shrugged. "You hang out in enough bars and you see these kinds of fights all the time. If someone doesn't get between them, they'll be trying to kill each other in a minute."

No sooner were the words out of his mouth than fists started flying. Peyton gasped. Crap, she might write about people fighting in her books, but she'd never seen one in real life. Beside her, Noah cursed under his breath.

He caught the eye of the guy manning the valet stand. "You might want to call hotel security. This is going to get out of hand quickly."

Peyton cringed as the one man shoved the

other to the ground, then jumped on top of him and started punching him in the face.

"Um, I'm not sure we can wait for security," she said. "Maybe you should go over there and do something before they get to the part where they actually kill each other."

Noah snorted. "And leave you here by yourself? I don't think so."

"The valet attendant is right here. I'll be fine." She made a face as she looked around him at the two men brawling. "Those guys might not be. One of them is already bleeding."

Noah scowled and glanced over his shoulder, then cursed again. "Stay right here."

Peyton nodded, but Noah was already striding toward the men fighting.

Noah reached down and jerked the bigger man off the top of the slightly smaller one, shoving him back from the fight. Then he bent down and helped the other guy off the ground. Peyton hoped that would be the end of it, but both guys went right back at each other, forcing Noah to get between them.

Where the heck is hotel security?

She glanced toward the hotel entrance, not understanding why there wasn't anyone on the way.

She was so focused on the door she didn't notice when a van squealed into the circular driveway and slammed on its brakes a few feet away. She jerked her head around in time to see a man in jeans, a dark sweatshirt, and a ski mask jump out the side door of the vehicle.

Peyton instinctively backed away, her heart suddenly pounding. She didn't know how she knew the guy was coming for her, but she did.

She screamed Noah's name at the same time she turned to run toward him, but Ski Mask grabbed her around the waist, picking her up off her feet and dragging her toward the van. She punched at the man's arm at the same time she tried to elbow him in the ribs. That always worked in her books, but this guy didn't even budge.

"Noah!"

He was already sprinting toward her, but it was too late. Ski Mask had already dragged her into van. The man fell backward with her into the vehicle, not bothering to even close the door as he held her tight and yelled at the driver to go. She screamed and struggled with all her might, terrified of what these men might do to her once they had her away from Noah.

The van rocked as it started to speed away

from the hotel, but before she could do more than take another gulp of air to scream again, there was a blur of movement, then Noah was in the vehicle with her and the man still clasping her around the waist. She had no idea how he'd caught up to the speeding van—or what he was going to do now that he was in it—and she really didn't care. He was here. Nothing else mattered.

Then Noah was leaning over her. One hand came up to gently move her head to the side as his other hand came down in a fist to whistle by her face and smash into Ski Mask's jaw. The guy's head bounced off the floor of the van, his arm relaxing around her waist.

Noah lunged forward and punched the driver in the back of the head, then tossed Ski Mask out the side door. Without a word, Noah wrapped his arms around her and jumped out of the still moving vehicle.

Peyton thought she might have screamed—she wasn't sure. All she knew was that she was prepared for a lot of pain the moment they hit the ground. The van hadn't been moving too fast as it spun through the parking lot and out onto the road, but it sure as heck wasn't standing still, either.

When the impact with the ground came, it didn't hurt at all. That was only because Noah had wrapped himself around her so that he hit the pavement instead of her. She stayed safely tucked in his protective embrace until they came to a tumbling stop. She was still lying on his chest, looking around in confusion as he sat up with her.

"Are you okay?" he asked urgently. "You aren't injured?"

She was shaken but moved her arms and legs, looking to see if anything hurt—nothing did. She shook her head. "I think I'm okay. How about you? I fell right on top of you."

He smiled at her as he stood, gently pulling her upright. "That's kind of the way I planned it."

She couldn't believe how calm Noah sounded after everything that had happened, and she found herself scanning his body for injuries. He seemed like he'd made it through the tumble without a single scratch—all except for his suit, of course, which hadn't fared so well—but then she noticed that he was standing a little gingerly and not putting any weight on his left leg.

"Crap," she said. "Did you hurt your knee again?"

"Just tweaked it a little running after you," he said. "I don't think I did any more damage to it."

Noah probably would have said more, but he was interrupted by the sound of running footsteps. She looked up and saw two men in suits and ties coming toward them with bewildered expressions on their faces.

"Hotel security," the taller of the two men said. "Are you two okay? What the hell just happened?"

Noah glanced at the pair as he gestured with his thumb toward the man in the ski mask lying unconscious on the sidewalk a few yards away.

"Call the cops," he said. "That asshole tried to kidnap Peyton Matthews. And if those two men who were fighting by the valet desk are still there, keep it that way. I'm pretty sure they're involved."

Peyton hadn't even considered those two idiots might have been a distraction, but now that she thought about it, the idea made sense.

The pair from hotel security looked down at the man, then one pulled out his cell phone while the other headed back to the valet desk. Ski Mask hadn't hit the ground as smoothly as she and Noah. One arm was bent at an odd angle. Then again, the guy might have been unconscious before he went out the door. That could have something to do with how poorly he'd landed.

She felt an arm come around her shoulders as Noah guided her away from the man who'd tried to grab her.

"Are you sure you're okay? Did that son of a bitch hurt you?"

Peyton shook her head. That was when it hit her. She'd almost been kidnapped. Noah had been right to worry all along. They hadn't tried to grab the hard drive or even her purse. They'd come after her.

"No, I'm fine." She gazed up at Noah, her voice suddenly clogging with tears as she realized how horrible this could have turned out. "You were right. About someone coming after me again to get my book. I mean. If you hadn't stopped them..."

"Shh," he whispered, smoothing her hair back with his hand. "You're okay. That's all that matters."

He brushed his thumb tenderly across her lips and for a moment, she thought he was going to kiss her, but instead he pulled her into his arms and held her close. She hugged him back, resting her cheek against his suit jacket. His heart beat steadily beneath her ear and she closed her eyes, smiling a little as she listened to the rhythmic sound. Being in his arms felt like the place she was supposed to be. Like the place she was *meant* to be. And if that sounded like something out of a romance book, she didn't care.

"What happened?"

Peyton reluctantly opened her eyes to see Gwen rushing toward them, followed closely by Claire, Kiki, Hannah, and Scott. All five stared at the man on the ground before looking at her and Noah.

"What happened?" Gwen asked again.

Peyton stepped a little away from Noah so she could turn to look at them. "Two guys tried to kidnap me," she said softly. "They would have succeeded too, if Noah hadn't stopped them."

Scott's eyes darted to Noah, then back to her. "Did they get the book?"

Noah glared at him, and Peyton thought he might punch Scott. "Two men tried to kidnap Peyton and all you care about is some damn book?"

Scott flushed and started to stutter something, but Gwen interrupted with a sharp look in his direction.

"No, definitely not. Peyton is our first concern."

Noah's jaw tightened. He didn't look like he believed that. And in that moment, Peyton wasn't sure she did, either. She wasn't naive. She knew that she was only as valuable to her publisher as her book series made her. But still, it was painful to see the reality of that fact presented so clearly.

"They didn't get the book," she told them quietly, patting the big purse that had stayed on her shoulder the whole time.

At least Scott had the grace not to show his relief as openly as Gwen and the others. Her editor looked like she wanted to say something, but two cop cars pulled into the hotel driveway then, their lights flashing. Two uniformed officers got out of the patrol car, whilc a plainclothes detective stepped out of the unmarked vehicle that pulled up behind them.

Peyton immediately recognized Dwayne Harrison, the tall detective who'd showed up at her house the night of the break-in. The man glanced at the bad guy still unconscious on the ground for a second before turning her way.

"I heard dispatch mention your name and figured this was something I needed to be involved in," the detective said. "Any chance this is related to the earlier break-in at your home?"

Peyton started to answer, but Noah beat her to it. "Almost certainly. She was doing a well-advertised book signing at the hotel and was carrying her computer hard drive in her purse. It was pure luck that I was able to stop the jackasses from getting away with Peyton and the book."

The detective looked at Noah, his eyes widening in surprise, then he smiled. "Noah Bradley? How the hell are you? More importantly, what the hell are you doing here?"

Noah grinned and reached out to clasp the man's outstretched hand "I'm good. And as far as what I'm doing here...well...it's complicated."

The man snorted. "When is anything in your life not complicated?"

"You two know each other?" Peyton interrupted, even though the answer was obvious.

Noah chuckled. "Are you telling me you don't recognize Dwayne from the photos you saw at my place?"

Peyton searched the detective's face as she tried to remember the people in the pictures at Noah's apartment. When the answer hit her, all she could wonder was why she hadn't recognized the man the moment she'd seen the photo.

"He's one of the guys you pointed out," she

said. "One of your Teammates who got out of the Navy!"

"Well, it's been a few years since I took that picture." Dwayne laughed. "And I might have added a few pounds, too, but I'll never admit that out loud to anyone else."

Peyton knew she couldn't ask what kind of injury the man had sustained while in the Navy because that would be seriously inappropriate. But she definitely wanted to know how this man had gone from being a Navy SEAL to a detective in the SDPD. Unfortunately, this didn't seem to be the time to talk about the man's past.

"You going to tell me what happened here?" Dwayne asked, gesturing to the woozy man the uniformed cops were helping sit up, then the two guys who'd been fighting earlier that hotel security was leading their way. "Because it looks like it was interesting."

Noah gave his former Teammate a quick rundown of what happened, starting with the fact that he'd been guarding Peyton since the break-in. Then he pointed out how the two men fighting had been there as a distraction so the guys in the van would get a clean shot at Peyton. She was stunned when Noah gave his friend a partial on the van's license plate. She had no idea how he'd been able to see it while running down the vehicle, but she was glad he had.

Dwayne immediately got on the radio and put out a BOLO on the car, then started asking more detailed questions. The first one was simple since he yanked the ski mask off the man who'd tried to grab Peyton and asked if she recognized him. She didn't. After that, he asked the two morons who'd been fighting by the front door what they had to say. Peyton expected them to immediately demand a lawyer—they always did on the TV shows—but instead, both men pointed at Ski Mask as the cops put him in the back of the police car.

"He paid each of us two hundred dollars to start a fight out front when she came out the door," one of them said, pointing at Peyton. "He told us it was some staged promotional event kind of thing."

Dwayne shook his head and motioned at the uniformed officers to take the men downtown for further questioning.

"Let me know when you pick up the driver," Noah said to Dwayne. "It would make my job easier once I know that guy is off the streets."

His friend nodded. "No problem. I'll be in touch."

Gwen, Scott, and the rest of her publisher's entourage had already given their statements—not that they'd seen anything since they were inside the hotel and had only heard about it after the fact.

"I'll stop by to check on you tomorrow," Gwen told Peyton, then looked at Noah. "Thank you for keeping her safe. I don't even want to think about what would have happened if those men had kidnapped her."

Noah looked like he wanted to say something suitably sarcastic in response, but Peyton caught his hand and gave it a squeeze. It was after midnight and she was too tired for this.

"This isn't over," Noah said. "Not until the cops catch that other guy."

Peyton only hoped that was soon.

CHAPTER

I FEEL HORRIBLE TAKING YOUR BED," PEYTON SAID AS THEY walked into his apartment. "If you had to sleep on my couch when you were staying at my place, shouldn't I get the couch at yours?"

"I slept on the couch at your place because it put me between your bedroom and the easiest way into your house," he said, taking off his suit jacket and tossing it over the back of the couch. "I'm sleeping on the couch here for the same reason. Anyone coming in the front door will have to go through me first before they can get to you."

Picking up her bags from where he'd set them down on the floor, he headed for his bedroom. It was probably an indication of just how rattled Peyton still was by the kidnapping attempt that she didn't even try to argue the point. Just like she hadn't complained when he suggested staying at his place instead of hers. She'd simply packed an overnight bag as fast as she could, grabbed her laptop and a yoga DVD, then followed him out the door.

Trying to grab her right in front of a crowded hotel in the middle of town was an act of desperate men. Someone—maybe even Magpie—was pushing to get Peyton's book sooner rather than later. And with one of the would-be thieves already in police custody, the other had to know he was running out of time. He'd come for Peyton as soon as he figured out where she was. Which meant keeping her somewhere they wouldn't expect.

"Do you have someplace I can set up my laptop?" she asked, following him into the bedroom. "I came up with a few thoughts for the ending of the book while doing the signing and I need to get them down before I forget what they are."

Noah turned to see her looking around, her gaze resting on his king size bed and the thick comforter spread across it. He wondered if he should point out that it was nearly midnight but knew it wouldn't matter. Peyton might be physically exhausted after the evening she had, but mentally, she was probably pinging off the walls. He wouldn't be surprised if she ended up staying awake half the night.

Adrenaline could do that to people who weren't used to it.

"You're more than welcome to pile up the pillows and write in bed," he said. "Or you can use the desk I have in the guest room. I have a home office set up in there, along with my workout equipment."

"I think I'll try the office," Peyton said. "If I write in bed, I'm afraid I'll end up falling asleep."

Noah quickly cleaned off the paperwork scattered around the desk and was shoving his weightlifting gear aside so she wouldn't feel so crowded when a knock at the door made him freeze. From the corner of his eye, he saw Peyton tense.

"Relax," he said softly. "If it was the bad guys, I doubt they'd knock. It's probably one of the guys bringing us leftover pizza. I sent them a text earlier, letting them know we'd be staying at my place."

Her shoulders dropped down from where they'd been crowding her ears even as another knock came, this one more insistent.

"I'd better get that before whoever it is gets worried and kicks in the door," he muttered.

Peyton flipped open her laptop with a smile

and slid into the office chair, her fingernails clicking over the keyboard before he barely made it out of the room. He couldn't imagine being creative enough to sit down and start typing like that. But that was what made her a writer and him not.

He felt the slightest twinge in his left knee as he walked across the living room. Considering how hard he'd gone after that van, he was lucky it wasn't worse. He could have blown out his knee completely.

Not that it would have stopped him. When he'd heard Peyton scream and turned to see some asshole dragging her into the back of a van, his heart seized in his chest. He'd run after the vehicle as fast as he could, his only concern getting to her in time.

It wasn't until they'd been lying on the sidewalk, his arms wrapped tightly around her, that Noah realized he was in trouble. At some point during the release party, he'd convinced himself that he was going to walk away when this was over. It was obvious that Peyton wasn't suited to being involved with a SEAL and getting out of Dodge was the smart thing to do. It would save both of them the trouble—and heartache—of watching everything fall apart later.

But after rescuing her from that pair of kidnappers, he realized he couldn't walk away from her. Not in a million frigging years. She'd already burrowed into his heart too deep to let her go.

He was still thinking about what that all meant when he yanked open the door and found his chief standing there.

Crap.

Chasen knows.

That was the only thing that made sense. Somehow...his boss had figured out he was working as Peyton's bodyguard and was here to rip him a new one.

"Is Peyton okay?" Chasen asked, stepping past him and into the apartment.

Noah stared at him. "What?"

"The kidnapping attempt at the Bayfront was all over the eleven o'clock news," he said, as if it should have been obvious. "Hayley's coworkers at the *Daily News* were calling every five minutes hoping I'd give them inside information on the Navy SEAL who kept the city's most famous author from getting abducted. Since you're seeing Peyton, it wasn't difficult to figure out you went to the signing with her and put yourself in the middle of everything, exactly like I'd expect you to do."

Noah breathed a sigh of relief. Chasen didn't know anything about the bodyguard gig. It sucked that word of the kidnapping attempt had made the news, though. He hadn't even considered that.

"You could have texted me," Noah said. "How did you even know I'd be here? I could just as easily have been at Peyton's place."

It was Chasen's turn to laugh as he cocked his head to the side and listened to the sound of rapid clicking from down the hallway as Peyton typed at a furious pace.

"You know I'm not a fan of texting when something is better done in person," his chief pointed out. "And as far as knowing you'd be here, that's easy. Peyton was threatened. It's only natural to bring her somewhere you consider home turf, so you can keep her safe."

Noah considered that. Chasen had put his recent actions into words far better than he'd ever be able to do.

"Is she okay?" Chasen asked again. "I hear typing going on in there, so I assume so."

"She's okay," Noah said softly, not wanting Peyton to overhear them talking about her. "A little rattled, but physically fine. She's dealing with it a lot better than I thought she would, considering how close she came to being kidnapped."

Chasen crossed his arms over his chest with a frown. "You think this was a one-time, random thing or an indication of something more?"

Part of Noah wanted to tell his boss about the true threat Peyton was facing. That someone—maybe Magpie—was after the manuscript of her next book and that he'd been protecting her ever since the break-in at her place. But there was no way in hell he could tell Chasen any of that. Not if he wanted to keep protecting Peyton.

"Her publisher thinks it was a one-time thing," he lied smoothly and feeling like crap for doing it. "It's probably because she has a book releasing next week. But I still felt better with her staying with me for a while."

"Makes sense," Chasen said with a nod. "But you have to admit, it's a little quick, isn't it? I mean, you've only known her for a couple days, right? It there something serious going on between the two of you?"

Noah almost denied it out of instinct, but then he realized Chasen probably already knew the answer to the question before he'd asked.

"Yeah, there is," he admitted quietly. "On my

part at least. I don't know if Peyton feels the same way. Or whether she's willing to explore it if she does. I think my being a SEAL might scare her off."

Chasen was silent for a moment, an understanding expression on his face. Like he knew exactly what Noah was going through. Which he did. Looking for someone to share their lives with while doing a job that asked so much, not only from them but everyone around them, was the same thing every one of his Teammates had to deal with.

"You can't hold it against her," Chasen said. "If she doesn't want to deal with it, I mean. Expecting a woman to live with thc kind of stress our career choice puts on her is a big ask for anyone. At the end of the day, all you can do is let her make the choice. But if she decides to try, it's on you to give her everything you have. At least everything the job will let you give her. Make sure she knows how much you care about her and that she's important to you."

They talked for a few more minutes, focusing on far less weighty matters than his potential relationship with Peyton or the danger that had her spending the foreseeable future at his place. The conversation centered on Noah's knee and assurances that he was maintaining his physical therapy schedule and not doing anything that would jeopardize his recovery.

Noah promised he was being a good little SEAL. Outside of running down the occasional kidnapping vehicle, of course.

When Chasen left, Noah stood for a moment in the middle of his living room, wondering why it was so quiet. It took him a moment to realize he couldn't hear the click of computer keys. Had Peyton fallen asleep at her keyboard?

He wandered down the hallway, stunned when he looked in the bedroom door and found her lying in the middle of the floor staring up at the ceiling intently. He stood there for a moment, waiting for her to see him, but whatever she was thinking about must have been damn interesting because she didn't notice him until he pushed away from the door jamb he'd been leaning against. She started, turning her head his way, and he immediately felt like crap for making her jump.

"Sorry." He offered her a smile with his apology. "I didn't mean to startle you. I wanted to let you know that it was Chasen at the door. He heard about the kidnapping attempt and wanted to make sure we were okay."

"Oh. That was nice of him," she said, clearly still preoccupied. "Thanks."

Noah wanted to ask if everything was cool, but when she went back to staring at the ceiling, he figured it would be better to let her work through whatever it was she was thinking about on her own.

"Wait!" Peyton said when he turned to leave.

He turned back around to see her standing in the middle of the room, her hand outstretched toward him.

"I could really use your body right now," she said.

It was quite possible his jaw dropped. Noah couldn't be sure because the rush of images that popped into his head right then made rational thought damn near impossible. He'd had women throw themselves at him before, but it usually happened after hanging out in a bar for a couple of hours. Never in a situation like this, and never as blatant and as matter of fact as this. He didn't know how to respond.

"Can you get on the floor with me?" she asked.

He opened his mouth, then closed it, not

sure where this version of Peyton had come from. She wasn't acting normal. Or at least not what he'd come to think of as normal for her. Could this simply be a reaction to what happened tonight? Had almost getting kidnapped made her decide to do something she'd usually never consider?

He took a deep breath. "I know you went through a lot earlier, but I'm not sure it's a good idea to jump into this. I wouldn't want you regretting it in the morning."

Peyton frowned, clearly confused. She looked at him for a few seconds before her eyes went wide.

"Oh! You thought I meant..." A rosy blush colored her cheeks. "I wasn't saying I wanted to have sex with you."

He lifted a brow, wondering if he should laugh or be offended. That only made her blush more.

"Crap, that didn't come out right! Of course, I'd have sex with you. What woman wouldn't?"

If putting your foot in your mouth was an Olympic event, Peyton would win a gold medal for sure. She must have figured that out, too, because her face started heading for beet-red.

"Double crap! That didn't come out right, either." She sighed and ran a hand through her long, blond hair in a gesture that was seriously sexy. "Let me start over before I say something I'm really going to regret. I asked you to get on the floor with me because I suck at writing fight scenes and the end of this book has a really big one that's giving me even more trouble than most. I thought you might be able to help me if we acted it out together."

It was his turn to be embarrassed. Talk about jumping to conclusions. Though he had to admit, while there was part of him relieved Peyton wasn't throwing herself into bed with him as a way to forget the earlier trauma, another part couldn't help but feel disappointed. It was a stupid thought—one he fought to shove aside as quickly as he could—but no matter how hard he tried, the disappointment was still there.

"It was a silly idea," Peyton added before he could respond, clearly embarrassed as hell now. "Forget I asked."

She started toward her computer, but he stopped her with a gentle touch on her arm. Now she was making him feel bad about jumping to the wrong conclusion in the first place.

"It's not silly. I'd be happy to help you."

Peyton caught her lower lip between her teeth, a move as sexy as running her hand through her hair—maybe more. "You don't mind?"

"No, not at all." He grinned. "What do you want me to do?"

She thought a moment. "In the scene, the hero and the other guy are fighting on the floor, but I can't figure out how the hero gets the knife away from him. Can you lie on the floor on your back?"

"Sure."

Noah walked into the center of the room and sat down on the carpet, then leaned back. "Like this?" She nodded. "And where are you?"

Peyton knelt down beside him, then straddled his legs, careful to make sure her dress didn't ride up too high. "Right here."

O-kay.

He supposed he should have seen that coming since she'd asked him to get down on the floor with her. But damn, with her on top of him like this, the last thing he was thinking about doing was choreographing a fight scene.

"So, I have the knife and you're trying to keep me from stabbing you," she said.

Peyton clasped her hands together and lifted them over her head like she was holding a weapon, then lowered them as if she were going to stab him. Noah automatically lifted both arms to block the downward thrust, then immediately slipped his hands sideways until he could wrap them gently around her wrists. The move was pure instinct, but his next thoughts weren't. Because all he could suddenly think about was how slender those wrists were, exactly like the rest of her. And her skin was so soft.

"This is as far as I got," she explained. "Any tips on what the hero should do?"

It was difficult to answer with her warm body practically lying on top of his. His cock stirred in his slacks. He ignored it. As much as any man can ignore a hard-on. "Are these guys experienced fighters? Do they have any special training?"

She shook her head, the ends of her hair brushing his shirt. "Not really. They're both on the football team, though."

Noah thought a minute, trying not to let himself get distracted by the way her breasts rose every time she took a breath.

"There are a few things the hero could do." Noah took his right hand away from her wrists, shifting the left so he could hold both of them in that one. "He could punch the other guy in the jaw or the ribs. Or he could buck up to get the other guy off balance and roll him off."

Her perfectly arched brows furrowed. "I'm not sure what you mean."

Realizing it was easier to show her, Noah lifted his hips suddenly to throw her off balance, then rolled both of them over until he was the one on top. He felt a slight twinge in his knee at the move, but nothing too bad. So, he focused on the move, reaching out to gently pin her wrists to the floor over her head.

Peyton blinked up at him, her blue eyes wide, her mouth slightly parted. Her lips were the color of strawberries. He bet they'd taste just as sweet. If he leaned over a little bit more, he could kiss her and see if he was right. It'd be so easy.

And stupid.

The cock straining against the front of his pants didn't agree. Crap. All he needed was for her to realize he was sporting wood.

Noah cleared his throat. "You can have the hero pin down both hands like I'm doing or just the one with the knife. Either way, from this point, it would be easy for him to punch the bad guy in the face a few times, then yank the knife away."

Peyton nodded, her expression a little confused, leaving Noah unsure as to whether she'd heard anything he said. Instead, she gazed up at him, the heat in her eyes making him think of nothing but kissing her. But he couldn't do that. It would only make a complicated situation more difficult.

"I should probably let you get back to writing," he said, trying to ease his weight off her enough to ensure Peyton wouldn't feel his hard-on rubbing up against her.

Something he thought might be disappointment flickered across her face, but it disappeared too quickly for him to be sure. She licked her lips once, then nodded.

He released her wrists, then reluctantly pushed himself to his feet. The sight of her lying on the floor, one leg bent at the knee, her skirt riding up her thighs was nearly his undoing, and it took everything in him not to get back down there with her and do what his body was begging him to do.

He swallowed hard and held out his hand to help her up. She placed her smaller one in his, allowing him to tug her to her feet. While she was tall, she still only came up to his chin, and she tilted her head back to gaze up at him.

"Thanks for helping me with the fight scene," she said.

He smiled. "Sure."

Peyton caught her bottom lip between her teeth as she nodded. Then she hesitated, as if she was thinking about saying something else, but didn't.

"I...um...I'll be out in the living room," he said.

Allowing his gaze to linger once more on those luscious lips of hers, Noah turned and left the room. He walked into the kitchen on autopilot, opening the fridge and staring at the contents as if he'd find something to distract himself from thoughts of Peyton and what nearly happened. Unfortunately, a few bottles of beer and the usual collection of condiments weren't interesting enough to manage that, so he guessed he was screwed.

CHAPTER
Twelve

After spending thirty minutes on the phone assuring a frantic Laurissa that she and Noah were fine and she was staying at his place, Peyton sent a text to Gwen letting her know where she could find her if she wanted to stop by the next day, then stripped off her dress and stepped into Noah's shower. She turned on the water and waited for it to warm up, thinking about the scene she just wrote. Truthfully, she was surprised she'd gotten any writing done at all. Not after how turned on she got from that little role-playing game on the floor.

She couldn't believe how close she'd come to wrapping her arms and legs around Noah and dragging him down for a kiss. It was only the thought of how embarrassed she'd be if Noah rejected her that stopped her. He might have gotten as aroused as she had during their pretend tussle—because there'd been no mistaking the hard-on pressing against her—but from how hesitant he'd been to get on the floor with her in the first place—not to mention how fast he wanted to get away from her afterward—it was obvious he didn't want their relationship going any further.

To say she was hurt and disappointed was the understatement of a lifetime. Which was probably insane. She had no business even thinking they had a chance, not with all the crap stacked against them. With his job as a SEAL and her schedule as a writer, there was no way this could work. They both knew it.

But if that was the case, why did she feel so crappy about it?

Once the water was at the perfect temperature, Peyton opened the bottle of shower gel and squeezed some of it into her hand. The scent of pineapples and coconut filled her nose as she ran the fragrant suds over her arms and down her legs.

Being on the floor with Noah earlier had been the closest she'd been to having sex in a while. Her desire had only intensified when he'd rolled over and pinned her hands to the floor. She'd never been one for kinky stuff in the bedroom, but that subtle show of dominance had gotten her seriously hot and bothered. Even now, she was getting tingly in all the right places merely thinking about it.

And if the bulge in his pants offered any indication, Noah had been as aroused as she was.

She rinsed off the soap, letting her hands linger on her breasts for a moment before gliding down to the juncture of her thighs. She was about half a second away from pleasuring herself when she remembered that she wasn't in her bathroom at home and that Noah was down the hall in the living room.

Stifling a moan at the thought of Noah knowing she was touching herself, Peyton shut off the water and stepped out of the shower. The towel made her already sensitive nipples ache even more and she couldn't resist giving them a squeeze as she dried off. Letting down her hair, she ran a brush through it, wrapped the towel around her body, then slipped stealthily into the hallway and the bedroom beyond. She changed into her usual shorts and tank top, then went out to say goodnight to Noah.

The TV was on ESPN, but the volume was turned down to almost nothing and Noah seemed more interested in the phone in his hands than *SportsCenter*. He must have caught sight of her, because he looked up, and Peyton was keenly aware of his gaze as she walked into the kitchen and grabbed a glass from the nearest cabinet. She messed with the controls on the front of the fridge, getting crushed ice, then filling the rest of the glass with water. Out of the corner of her eye she saw him watching her, his attention making her suddenly warm all over.

Peyton stopped at the archway between kitchen and living room, leaning her shoulder there and gazing at Noah with a casualness she didn't really feel. Hadn't she come out to say good night? Why was she standing here practically blushing from the heat of Noah's smolder?

"Did the writing go well?" he asked, leaning forward to place his cell phone on the coffee table. He was still wearing his shirt and dress slacks and Peyton couldn't remember when she'd ever seen a man look so sexy.

Peyton nodded, not interested in talking about her book. Not when there were other things—much better things—to discuss.

"Did you want something to eat?" he asked, his expression betraying his confusion at her silence. "I know it's late, but I have some frozen pizza if you want to pop it in oven."

She took a sip of water before answering. "No, I'm good. If I tried to eat anything this late, I'd never fall asleep."

He nodded and silence filled the space around them again. But it was a comfortable silence, at least for her. She could stand there looking at him for hours and not feel the need to say anything.

But that would only be a waste of both of their times, wouldn't it?

Noah had told her he wanted to see if they could be more. Then he'd told her the last thing he wanted to do was let her get hurt by falling for him when she wasn't ready for what it meant to be with a man like him. He'd been the one brave enough to put it out there for her. He'd only started pulling back when it seemed like she wasn't going to reciprocate with the same level of bravery. Like she wasn't willing to take a chance.

If she wanted to see where this could go with Noah, she was going to tell him that. And she needed to do it now.

"I want to give us a chance," she said softly, then hurried on, hoping the right words would find a way to come out. "I'm scared of falling for you and then finding out that I'm not strong enough to deal with everything that comes with that. But I'm even more terrified of letting this slip away and then spending the rest of my life regretting it. So, if you're willing to give it a shot, then so am I."

Noah didn't say anything, and for one horrifying moment, Peyton was sure she'd read the entire situation wrong. That Noah had backed off because he wasn't interested in her. That she'd embarrassed herself and ruined everything.

Then her big SEAL bodyguard stood, closing the distance between them in a blur. She expected him to stop a few feet away, to look her deep in the eyes and say he was ready to take a chance, too. But he didn't stop, and he didn't speak. Instead, he pulled her into his arms and kissed her until a moan of pleasure found its way up from deep in her chest.

Peyton guessed that was Noah's way of saying yes.

Peyton had read more than a few romance books that included lines about the heroine being kissed until she felt breathless and dizzy. Having never experienced anything like that herself, she took it for nothing more than romantic prose and avoided it in her own stories. But by the time Noah stepped back to look down at her, his eyes smoldering with heat, she was definitely out of breath and lightheaded, leaving her with the amazing realization that sometimes romance books got it right.

"Where do we go from here?" Noah asked softly, resting his forehead on hers, his arms around her.

She smiled up at him. "How about your bedroom?"

He continued to gaze down at her. "Are you sure? We don't need to rush anything. Now that I know you're in this with me, I can wait forever if I have to."

Peyton went up on tiptoe and silenced whatever else he might be about to say with a kiss. Then she put her arms around his neck, in case he got any ideas about pulling away again. He didn't even try. Instead, he slid one hand into her hair and settled the other on the small of her back, tugging her close.

She moaned against his mouth, letting his tongue take possession of hers and teasing her mercilessly. Desire spiraled through her, making her tingle. Maybe it was everything that happened tonight—the way he'd risked himself to save her life, the fact that they were really committing to something long-term—but right then, Peyton wanted Noah more than she'd ever wanted anyone.

She slid her hands down his chest, the muscles there reminding her of how built he was underneath his dress shirt. "Take me to bed," she said softly.

He pulled back to gaze down at her for one long moment, then swung her up in his arms without another word and headed down the hall. She hooked her arms around his neck and rested her head against his shoulder. There was definitely something to be said for being with a big, strong guy.

When they got to his room, Noah carried her over to the bed and gently lowered her feet to the floor. Peyton immediately reached up and undid his tie, before using the ends to pull him close for another kiss. As their lips continued to move hungrily against each other, she worked her way down his shirt, fumbling a little with the buttons in her eagerness, but finally getting them undone.

Peyton took a few seconds to enjoy the feel of all those muscles under her hands as she pushed the dress shirt off his shoulders and down his arms. Then she ran her fingers slowly across his bare chest, pausing to appreciate every perfectly sculpted muscle along the way. There were some scrapes and bruises along the outside of one shoulder and down his back from where he'd hit the ground after jumping out of the van with her in his arms, but the wounds didn't seem to bother him at all.

She moved lower, lightly tracing his six-pack until she got to his belt. He caught her hands before she could tug it open. Peyton looked up at him in confusion.

Noah flashed her a sexy grin. "My turn."

Peyton arched an eyebrow, certainly not planning to protest as Noah reached down to grab the hem of her tank top and slowly pulled it up and over her head. Dropping her top casually to the floor, he stood there, his eyes worshiping every inch of bare skin, his gaze slowing as it slid over her breasts. He locked on the rosy tips, the heat in his eyes making her burn hot all over as he moved closer and caught his fingers in the waistband of her shorts. Lips edging up at the corner, he nudged them down over her hips, letting them fall to the floor and leaving her standing there naked.

"You're so beautiful," Noah said as he cupped her breasts, his thumbs teasing her nipples and making her gasp.

Peyton grasped his shoulders, afraid she might fall if she didn't. A moment later, she was glad she had because Noah bent and closed his mouth around one sensitive peak. She caught her breath. Oh yeah, if she weren't holding onto something right then, she would have definitely floated away—or melted into a puddle on the floor.

He suckled on her breasts, going back and forth from one to the other until she could barely think straight. She didn't know if it was possible to orgasm from what he was doing, but she definitely wouldn't mind finding out.

But Noah stopped before she could.

Peyton opened her eyes to find him regarding her, a smile tugging at his lips.

"I could do that all night," he said. "But if I did, then I wouldn't get to taste the rest of your gorgeous body."

Before she could reply, his mouth covered hers and he was urging her back onto the bed, until her knees hit the edge and she tumbled onto the mattress. Then Noah was standing there at the side of the bed, gazing down at her completely naked body.

He never broke eye contact with her as he dropped to his knees by the bed. Then he grabbed her legs and pulled her closer to the edge of the mattress, getting her perfectly positioned. Peyton's breath hitched. Gaze locked with hers, he slowly ran his hands up the inside of her thighs before leaning forward and carefully spreading her legs. Then he leaned forward a little more and kissed the inside of her leg.

He moved down slowly, nibbling and kissing one millimeter at a time, teasing her until she thought she would go crazy. She could feel the warmth of his breath on her pussy long before his mouth ever actually touched her there.

But when he finally did, she was sure she would explode. She didn't, but she did moan and squirm around like a woman possessed. Noah wrapped his arms firmly around her thighs, holding her tightly as he teased her to the point of insanity.

She tried to get her fingers in his hair, so she could steer him where she needed him, but his hair was too dang short to get a grip on, and she was reduced to little more than unintelligible moans and demands, which he completely ignored.

Just when Peyton was sure she couldn't take the teasing even one more second, Noah moved his mouth up to her clit and flicked it with the tip of his tongue. Her response was immediate and intense.

She screamed, arched her back, and came.

The waves of her climax were so powerful it felt like every muscle in her body was spasming at the same time. She'd never experienced anything like it and wasn't completely sure she'd survive even this first time.

She did, bucking and jerking as Noah tugged every trace of pleasure from her body. By the time he was done, Peyton was panting for breath. She should have been exhausted after coming so hard—and for so long—but she wasn't. If anything, she felt more alive than she'd ever been.

When Noah got to his feet, Peyton gave him a smile and rolled onto her knees. "Okay, now it's my turn."

Noah didn't need any more encouragement. She waited impatiently for him to unbuckle his belt and take off his dress pants, but when he finally shoved down his boxer briefs, the reveal was worth it. His cock was as beautiful as the rest of him—long, thick, and hard. She leaned forward and took him into her mouth, teasing with her tongue and sighing how delicious he tasted.

He slipped his hand in her long hair, urging her to take more of him, but also controlling her movements at the same time. She alternated between teasing licks and deeper swallows until Noah pulled back with a husky groan. Peyton didn't complain. As much as she'd like to make him come this way, she needed him inside her even more. There would be time for other games later.

Giving her a sexy grin, Noah opened the drawer of the nightstand and took out a condom. She watched as he rolled it on, then slid higher up on the bed, settling himself between her legs. He was so big and strong above her and she loved watching his muscles flex as he braced himself on one arm while slowly slipping inside her. Then all she could focus on was how amazing he felt. He filled her completely and as they moved together,

her legs came up and wrapped around him, squeezing him tight and never wanting to let him go.

Noah pumped his hips slowly at first, his mouth coming down to cover hers with kisses that took her breath away. But soon, he began to move faster, his thrusts becoming more forceful. She tightened her arms and legs around him, urging him on even more, loving the feel of him moving inside her like this.

When she came, it was as mind-blowing as the first time, but this one felt even more special because Noah came with her, grunting as he buried his face in the curve of her neck and nipped her deliciously.

He thrust hard, plunging deep inside her and emptying himself completely. Then he flipped her over to rest comfortably on his chest. Being with him like this felt more right than anything in her life ever had.

CHAPTER
Thirteen

NOAH WOKE UP TO THE JARRING SOUND OF HIS PHONE ringing somewhere nearby. He rolled out of bed before his sleep-deprived mind got around to remembering his cell was out in the living room where he'd left it last night before carrying Peyton to bed.

He glanced over his shoulder at the amazing woman who'd totally flipped his world upside down last night. The sight of Peyton lying there with the sheet and blanket draped over her naked body, one hand reaching as if trying to recapture the warmth of his presence, took his breath away.

His phone rang again and he reluctantly dragged his gaze away from her and headed out of the bedroom. Noah wasn't sure how many times they'd made love last night. At least three, not counting the time they spent simply kissing.

He'd never experienced a night like it before. But as amazing as the lovemaking had been, it was entirely possible it had been the quiet moments of conversation in between that were the most memorable for him.

They'd talked about stuff both silly and serious, with topics ranging from books she hoped to write one day to exotic countries he wanted to take her to. Then he'd told Peyton about his work on the SEAL team. Nothing specific or classified, but he'd opened up and shared stories of some of the places he'd been and things he'd seen. The fact that he was able to talk to her about that part of his life—even if it was in a heavily censored kind of way—meant everything to him. It made him think that maybe this thing between them could work.

Noah found his phone on the coffee table where he'd left it, picking it up but not recognizing the number. He thumbed the button to answer it anyway. Too many people had his number to ignore the call.

"Bradley," he said quietly, not wanting to wake Peyton.

"Noah, it's Dwayne," came the rumble of a deep voice. "Sorry to call you so early, especially after the night you had, but I thought you'd want to know that we caught the other kidnapper from last night. Uniform officers are bringing him to the Central Division station as we speak."

That was the one part of last night he'd happily forget if he could. Just thinking about those assholes dragging Peyton into that van made his heart thump like a racehorse. Which was kind of crazy, considering all the near-death experiences he'd been through.

"How'd you catch the guy so fast?" he asked.

There was a chuckle from the other end of the phone. "Turns out our kidnapping suspect isn't the brightest bulb in the box. We found the van in a parking lot in Encanto. One of our K9 teams tracked the man right to his apartment complex less than four blocks away. We took him into custody without any problems as soon as he opened the door."

Noah would have thought the men who'd tried to kidnap Peyton were smarter than that. Knowing about her book and how valuable it would be on the black market implied they weren't the run-of-the-mill smash-and-grab types. Hell, having the connections to sell her manuscript once they'd gotten it should have put those guys in a different stratosphere.

"I thought you might want to be there when we talk to the guy, so you can reassure Peyton this thing is really over," Dwayne said, interrupting Noah's mental ramblings. "I got the feeling she'd believe it more coming from you than me and the SDPD."

Noah almost asked if his relationship with Peyton was that obvious, but decided the question wasn't necessary. He already knew what Dwayne would say.

"Actually, yeah, I would. Thanks." He glanced at the time on the DVR clock below his TV. "With traffic at this time of the morning, it will probably take me thirty of forty minutes to get to your part of town. Will that still work?"

"No problem," Dwayne said. "It will take at least that long to process him and get him into an interrogation room. Longer if he asks for a lawyer."

Noah got the directions for where he needed to go once he got to the Central Division station and then hung up, heading back to the bedroom.

Peyton was awake, one hand resting on the pillow behind her head, the position doing all kinds of amazing things to her already amazing breasts, which, as it turns out, weren't covered by the blanket. Like she'd been planning to seduce him or something.

"I'm guessing that was Detective Harrison?" she asked, casually stretching in the morning sun streaming through the window like a cat. If he thought her breasts had looked entrancing before, it was nothing compared to now. And yes, his cock certainly noticed. Which reminded him of the fact that he wasn't wearing a stitch of clothing.

The slight smile that tilted up the corners of her lips made him think Peyton had noticed him looking.

"Yeah, that was Dwayne."

He'd intended to head over to the dresser for his clothes, but instead found himself climbing into bed with her. Peyton shoved the sheets and blankets aside, making room for him and baring her entire body. Even after all the time he'd spent gazing at her last night, it was still impossible not to stare again.

"They caught the driver of the van from last night," he added. "Dwayne offered to let me be a fly on the wall while they questioned him."

"When do you need to leave?" she asked, trailing her hands across his chest, her nails lightly grazing the muscles of his pecs.

"Pretty much now," he admitted, hating the disappointed look that crossed her face. "I want to be there when they start talking to this guy and traffic is gonna be painful."

She sighed. "I'd go with you, but unfortunately, I still have a lot more writing to get done today."

Noah cursed himself for not including her in the trip down to the police station, assuming she wouldn't be interested. Something to check himself about in the future. *Make no assumptions.*

"I wouldn't even think about leaving you here alone if I thought you were in any danger," he said, not sure if he was trying to reassure himself or her. "For one thing, no one knows you're staying here, and for another, the people who were trying to get the book from you are now locked up. You'll be fine here until I get back."

Peyton seemed to accept that, but Noah still found himself curling the ends of her hair around his index finger. He was about to say something profound about always keeping her safe when Peyton leaned over and kissed him hard. Noah pulled her close, his hand finding its way deeper into her hair as he dragged his mouth away.

"I should go," he rasped out in between her kisses. "Dwayne is waiting for me."

She playfully nipped his lower lip, slowly wiggling her body on top of his. He was already hard before she even fully straddled him. "You'll only be a few minutes late. I promise it will be worth it."

He groaned, rolling her onto her back and kissed her again. "Did I ever tell you I like the way you think?"

"Okay, it's official," Peyton said into her phone as she sat on Noah's comfy couch. "I'm falling seriously hard for your brother. And no, you aren't getting any details about last night."

Laurissa laughed. "Trust me, I have no desire to hear them."

But just because Laurissa didn't want to discuss the private aspects of last night's adventures, that didn't mean she didn't want to hear everything else. So, while Peyton probably should have kept writing, she instead spent the next fifteen minutes telling her best friend everything that happened at his place after they got there, followed by a word-for-word recap of how she convinced Noah that they could have something real between them.

Laurissa practically swooned. "Man, if there was ever any doubt that you write romance for a living, it's gone now. Because that stuff you just told me was romantic gold. Please tell me it's going to find its way into one of your books soon, pretty please?"

Peyton was still laughing when the doorbell rang.

Startled, she stood up to move tentatively across the living room, wondering if she should simply ignore whoever it was. Then she remembered that Gwen was supposed to stop by.

"Someone's at the door," she said, interrupting her friend's ongoing monologue on Noah's habit of eating all the Oreo cookies when they were kids. "Hold on while I take a peek."

Fully expecting to see Gwen, she was a little surprised when she looked through the peephole and instead saw Scott standing there looking sweaty and uncomfortable as hell in his normal 5th Avenue wool suit. Not surprising since the temperature outside was probably already in the mid-90's.

"My editor is here," she said into the phone. "I'm going to have to call you back later."

"No worries," Laurissa said. "Tell my brother I said hi."

Promising she would, Peyton unlocked the door and opened it, stunned to see an older man in an expensive suit with Scott. He must have been standing off to the side for Peyton not to have seen him through the peephole. That worried her. These days, she didn't deal well with people she didn't know.

"Hope we didn't interrupt your writing," Scott said with a familiar smile that went a long way to calming her nerves. Scott was as much of a friend as an editor. If he brought someone with him, there was no reason not to trust the man. "Gwen would have come herself, but she got busy on some contract negotiations and asked me to come in her place," he added as Peyton stepped aside to let them in. "She also wanted me to introduce you to Daris Markovic. He's a prospective investor."

Peyton groaned silently. She knew very little about the business side of publishing but was fully aware that it took a lot of money. As one of the publisher's most well-known authors, she was always being paraded in front of people with fat bank accounts in the hopes of luring some money out of them.

"Nice to meet you, Mr. Markovic," she said, stepping forward to shake the dark-haired man's hand.

"Please, call me Daris," the man said with a warm smile. "Truthfully, my entire reason for approaching your publisher with an offer of investment was so I'd get a chance to meet you. I hope I don't embarrass you by admitting that I'm your biggest fan."

Peyton laughed. Impressing potential investors might not be her thing, but this she could handle. Daris was a fan. He simply had more money than most. And maybe he was a little outside the normal demographic, but that was okay, too.

She was about to ask if they wanted coffee, but the moment they sat down on the couch, Daris immediately peppered her with questions about her books. They spent the next few minutes talking about her series and the most recent book. Daris shocked her by admitting he'd already read every book in the series twice. Crap, he really was a fan!

Scott made a comment or two about the book, but she could tell he wasn't as into the conversation as Daris was. Peyton tried to ignore her editor's uncomfortable silence, but after a while that became impossible.

"Is everything okay, Scott?" she finally asked. "You seem quiet this morning."

Scott seemed to be caught off guard by the question. He flushed and dropped his gaze to stare down at the floor. She thought for a moment that he wasn't going to answer, but when he finally looked at her again, the expression of contrition on his face was hard to miss.

"I wanted to tell you how sorry I am about what I said last night," he said, giving her a sheepish look. "When I asked about the book before even checking to see if you were okay. I mean, I didn't intend to make it seem like I was more interested in your book than your safety."

She waved her hand, a little surprised Scott was fixated on something like that. "Don't worry about it. Things got a little crazy last night. But I'm fine, the book is fine, and the cops caught the jerks who tried to get it. I certainly don't hold your concern for the book against you. It's your job. So please, it isn't a big deal."

Scott let out a sigh, relaxing as if a great weight had been lifted from his shoulders. "Thanks. I appreciate that. Speaking of the book, I guess I should ask how it's coming. It's why Gwen sent me over in the first place."

"It's almost finished," she said, almost laughing at the look of surprise on Scott's face. "The only thing I have left to do is wrap up the ending, but I can't quite seem to get it the way I want it. It's lacking a certain punch, if you know what I mean? I'm trying to get the intensity to match the end of the previous books and it isn't quite there yet."

"Do you want me to take a peek?" Scott asked. "Maybe I could help you out."

"Sure," she said. He'd been pretty good at making suggestions when they'd worked together on the previous books. "I was about to get some coffee. Do you two want some?"

Scott looked over at Daris, who nodded. "That'd be great. Thanks."

"Cream and sugar?"

"That's good for me," Scott said while Daris asked for milk in his.

She pointed at the computer sitting on the coffee table with a smile. "The last page of the story is already up for you. I was working it when you knocked. Have a look and see what you think. You can take a look too, Daris. Just keep in mind that this is the rough draft and is likely to change a little in the final version."

She almost laughed at how fast Daris moved to grab a seat on the couch beside Scott, his excitement obvious. She watched the two men reading for a moment before heading to the kitchen, where she made fresh coffee and poured it into three mugs, adding cream, sugar, and milk as the men had asked. She wasted a few seconds looking for something she could use as a serving tray before giving up and picking up all three mugs at once to carry them back out to the living room. When she stepped out of the kitchen, she froze in the doorway.

While Daris was over by the shelves, looking at Noah's pictures, Scott was still by her computer, standing there with a flash drive in his hand and a guilty expression on his face, looking almost as shocked as she was.

"What the hell are you doing?" she demanded, already knowing the answer.

Out of the corner of her eye, she noticed Daris wasn't even looking at them, but it wasn't like she cared.

Scott flushed. "This isn't what it looks like."

She tightened her grip on the mugs. "Really? Because it looks like you're trying to steal my book."

Scott didn't say anything.

"That *is* what you were trying to do, isn't it?" she insisted. "Why would you do something like that?"

When he still didn't answer, Peyton thought maybe she was wrong. But then Scott's face twisted, looking angrier than she'd ever imagined it could be.

"Because I'm tired of being pissed on and told it's raining. I'm the one who scooped your first book off the slush pile all those years ago. I was the one who fought to get it on the table for consideration. I'm the one who stood up for you and the series at the acquisition meetings when everyone kept saying that young adult print sales were dead and gone. I got your series published. And I was the one who edited the first two books in the series, not Gwen. Hell, she was one of the people who didn't see any potential in the series. I was the one who put your books on the bestseller lists!"

Peyton frowned, stunned. Yes, she'd worked with him on her earlier books, but she had no idea he'd been the one who found it in the slush pile.

"But I thought you were getting promoted to full editor in the thriller market," she said softly.

"I thought so too, but then Gwen decided she needed my help too much to let me leave." He snorted. "I figured if I was going to do this much damn work on a book, I should at least get paid for it. Luckily, there are people like Daris around who recognize the true value I bring to the team. And what a book like yours can really be worth."

Peyton's stomach clenched as she put two and two together. She threw another quick glance toward Daris, to see that he was definitely interested in the conversation now. "You hired those guys to kidnap me?"

Scott shrugged. "I didn't pay for them, of course. That was Daris. But I did pick them out and tell them what to do. And they would have pulled it off too, if it wasn't for that stupid fucking Navy SEAL."

"A miscalculation on your part," Daris murmured from his place over by Noah's bookshelf with the framed photos.

Scott's lip curled. "How the hell was I supposed to know the publisher hired a damn Navy SEAL to be your bodyguard? And then you up and disappear after the signing at the hotel I thought for sure I'd never find you. I almost flipped when I overheard Gwen talking to the publisher about you staying with your bodyguard. Luckily, Daris had no problem finding the address."

This was insane. All this time she'd thought it was nameless, faceless criminals looking to sell her book to the highest bidder. Discovering it was someone she trusted made the whole thing even worse.

"You didn't think you could walk out of here with that flash drive without me knowing, did you?" she asked.

"Yeah, I did." He slowly slipped the flash drive into his pocket. "And if you'd come out of the kitchen a few seconds later, you never would have realized I'd made a copy. Truthfully, I really wish you hadn't caught me because now, I'm going to have to do something about it."

Peyton's blood ran cold. *Crap.* For the first time since she'd walked in here, she realized she might be in trouble.

Before she knew what she was even doing, Peyton threw the three mugs of hot coffee at Scott, turning to run for the door even as he let out a curse.

Daris caught her as she yanked the door open. She tried to fight him, but he grabbed her arm and spun her around. Her back slammed against the wall and her head hit with a thud. She was sure he was going to hit her, but before he got the chance, everything went black and she felt herself falling.

CHAPTER *Fourteen*

NOAH COULDN'T REMEMBER HAVING IT SO BAD FOR A woman before, but after spending one amazing night with Peyton, he knew she was in his blood forever. He hadn't been able to think about anything other than her the whole way to the police station. Hell, he was so preoccupied, he was damn lucky he hadn't driven off the road. Even now, as he strode inside the building and headed upstairs to see Dwayne, he was still daydreaming about how much fun that quickie had been with her this morning.

He knew he was probably grinning like an idiot as he finally found his friend's desk, but he didn't care. Peyton was the kind of woman who made him not give a crap what people thought of him.

Dwayne was reading something intently

on his computer screen when Noah walked up. "Finally. I was starting to think you weren't going to make it."

"Traffic was a nightmare," Noah said, berating himself for staying for that quickie even though he would never really be able to regret it. "Hope I didn't miss anything important."

"Not yet." Dwayne snorted. "As I suspected, the guy lawyered up immediately. But it looks like they're ready to make a deal. I was about to go talk to them. You still want to listen in, right?"

"Definitely."

Noah was interested in knowing what the asshole who tried to kidnap Peyton thought he might have to offer up for a deal, but he guessed he was about to find out.

"It goes without saying, but you were never officially here," Dwayne murmured as he led the way down a long narrow hallway. "You're here to observe only. Understood?"

"Hooyah," Noah said.

Stopping, Dwayne motioned him into a dimly lit room with a two-way mirror that allowed him to see into the interrogation room. The man Noah had tangled with last night was already sitting at a table, along with a second man who must have been his partner in crime. In between them sat a gray-haired guy in a suit whom Noah assumed was their lawyer. All three men sat up a little straighter when Dwayne walked in and took a seat opposite them.

"I understand your clients have something they want to tell me, Mr. Carpenter," Dwayne said to the gray-haired man.

Carpenter nodded. "In return for a deal, yes."

"You know how this works," Dwayne said. "Your clients talk and if I think the information is worth anything, the appropriate recommendations will be filed with the ADA. But it all depends on what they have to say."

Carpenter hesitated, then nodded at the two men.

The one who'd grabbed Peyton and dragged her into the van took a deep breath. Without the ski mask, he didn't look nearly as tough. "We were only trying to kidnap that writer because someone hired us to do it. We were never gonna hurt her. We were told to get an external hard drive from her, but she had a death grip on that frigging purse of hers."

Noah tensed. If someone had hired these two idiots, that person was still out there and would almost certainly go after Peyton and her book again.

"Who hired you?" Dwayne asked.

"Two men," the driver of the van said. "The one in charge—a dark-haired foreign-looking guy—never said a word. He just stood in the background and listened. The second one did all the talking. He had a New York accent and liked to talk loud, like he thought he was tough or something."

Dwayne frowned. "That doesn't really narrow it down. If you want a deal, you're going to have to do better than some foreign guy and a loud talker from New York. I need a name."

"They never used names," Getaway Driver said. "And before you ask, New Yorker paid up front in cash. Five thousand in cash—each. We thought at first there were some kind of military or industrial secrets on the hard drive, but New Yorker said it was a damn romance book if you can you believe that."

Dwayne ignored the meaningless commentary and stuck to the point. "Well, if you can't give me a name, how about a description?"

"New Yorker was white. Maybe five-ten in height. Blond hair," the second kidnapper answered. "The other one was older, maybe early fifties with dark black hair. Really expensive suit, though. Worth more than my car."

Noah clenched his jaw. Getaway Driver's description was about useless. They'd never be able to find anybody with information like that.

"Anything else you can remember about them?" Dwayne asked. "Tattoos or distinguishing characteristics?"

Both men were silent for a few moments before the first guy spoke again.

"It's not really a distinguishing characteristic, but New Yorker had this irritating habit of twirling a damn pen between his fingers all the time. It was distracting as crap."

Noah's gut clenched.

Shit.

He rapped on the one-way glass with his knuckles to get Dwayne's attention, then walked out of the room, hoping his friend got the message. Fortunately, he had.

"What's up?" Dwayne asked as he met Noah in the hallway.

"I know the son of a bitch who hired those guys," Noah told him. "The one they called New Yorker. It's one of the editors at her publisher by the name of Scott Moore. He's staying at the hotel where they had the release party last night."

"You sure it's him?"

"I'm sure. The description was dead on. He's one of the few people that knew she kept the book on a hard drive in her purse and he spent the whole night twirling his pen between his fingers," Noah said. "I'm going home to Peyton. Call me when you pick up Moore for questioning. I have no doubt your two suspects in there will ID him in a split second."

As he raced down the stairs, Noah pulled out his phone and hit the speed dial for Peyton. It rang four times, then went to voice mail.

Dammit.

"Peyton, it's me. I don't know exactly what's going on, but Scott Moore hired those two guys who tried to kidnap you. He's working with another man, but I don't know who. Don't open the door for anyone but me. I'm on my way."

Noah cranked his SUV and squealed out of the parking lot, only realizing he was in front of a police station at the last second. He forced himself to ease off the accelerator. He wouldn't do Peyton any good if the cops pulled him over. But the twenty minutes it took to get back to his apartment was pure agony. He called Peyton half a dozen more times, only to get her voice mail every time. In desperation he gave Sam a call, simply telling him that Peyton was in trouble and to get over to his apartment.

By the time he slid to a stop in the driveway of his apartment complex, Noah was close to losing his mind.

The door to his place was ajar, like someone had left in a hurry and hadn't bothered to make sure it was closed. Noah's heart froze and dread began to settle in the pit of his stomach even as he shoved open the door and stepped into the living room.

"Peyton!" he called out. "Where are you?"

He was met with complete silence.

Three mugs lying on the floor caught his attention, creamy coffee staining the carpet around them. A little further away, the coffee table had been shoved slightly out of position. Those were the only signs of struggle, but Noah didn't have to be a genius to figure out what happened. Moore and the dark-haired man had shown up at the apartment and talked their way in. Peyton had obviously trusted them enough to offer coffee, but then something had gone wrong. Since her laptop was on the table, it was almost a certainty that she'd caught the men trying to make a copy of the book or something like that.

A quick check confirmed that the stains on the floor were already cold and starting to dry. He hadn't been gone very long, so that meant this had all happened a while ago, maybe shortly after he'd left.

He moved through the rest of apartment quickly, terrified he'd find Peyton on the floor in another room lying in a pool of blood. Moore had struck him as kind of a wimpy guy, but who knew how he'd react if Peyton confronted to him. And the dark-haired guy was a total wild card.

"Peyton!" he called again, running down the hallway, past the smaller bedroom where he had his home office, then into the master bedroom. She wasn't in either.

The continued silence was deafening.

He paused long enough to open his gun safe and pull out the small frame 9mm Glock he always kept loaded there. He shoved the slim holster inside the waist of his jeans, then he was up and running down the hall.

On the way, he did a check of the bath, kitchen, and coat closest, confirming what he'd already suspected. Peyton wasn't there. Moore and the unknown dark-haired man must have taken her with him. Noah wasn't sure why, but it couldn't be anything good.

A noise at the door made him spin around, the 9mm coming up to center on the person stepping into the apartment. If it wasn't for his years of SEAL training that always hammered him on the importance of identifying his target before pulling the trigger, he probably would have killed his own teammate.

"Whoa, dude. It's just us." Sam held up his hands. "What the hell is going on? Where's Peyton? And why are you standing in the middle of your apartment with a gun in your hand?"

Noah lowered his weapon as Wes and Lane followed Sam into the apartment, all three of them looking around curiously.

Every instinct Noah had urged at him to run out of the apartment in a mad effort to find Peyton, but he needed to tell his buddies what was going on first. Keeping it brief, Noah told them what he'd learned at the police station that morning. As he filled them in on Moore and his partner, he didn't miss the looks that passed between his Teammates as he described the dark-haired man who'd apparently supplied the money to hire the kidnappers.

"We just got another intel briefing on Magpie this morning from Woods," Sam said. "They've confirmed the man is somewhere in the western United States and told us what he looks like. That dark-hair guy with Moore fits the description Woods gave us."

Noah considered that for a moment and realized that it made a lot of sense. Magpie was supposedly under a lot of pressure to come up with an immediate source of funding for terrorist operations. That pressure must have made him get personally involved in the acquisition of the largest source of funding available to him—Peyton's manuscript.

"Okay, if we think the dark-haired man with Moore is Magpie, how does that help us find Peyton?" Noah wondered aloud. "Why kidnap her if all they wanted was her book?"

He and his Teammates stood there arguing over the possibilities, running the gamut from Peyton already being dead—which Noah refused to consider—to Moore and Magpie taking Peyton alive in order to force her to write the next book in the series—which seemed unfeasible—to Peyton having left on her own to chase after the men who'd taken her book—an idea that seemed even more unlikely.

"Maybe it's as simple as Moore and Magpie taking Peyton with them as a hostage until they get away," Sam pointed out.

Noah had to admit that was the most likely scenario. "Okay, assuming they're interested in getting out of town, the question is, how?"

He was wondering if he should call Dwayne when Wes pulled out his phone. "I may be able to answer that."

A few seconds later, Noah heard him talking to Kyla, telling her what was happening and asking if she could hack into the security camera that monitored the border crossing points into Mexico, along with those at the ports, bus stations, and airports. It must be nice to have a girlfriend who could hack into anything even remotely electronic in nature. Which is why Navy Intelligence had hired her.

Noah had no idea what Kyla might come up with—and he wasn't sure he wanted to wait around and see—but Kyla called Wes back two minutes later.

"Scott Moore booked a one-way flight to Puerto Vallarta, Mexico earlier this morning on Southwest Airlines," Kyla said when Wes put her on speaker phone. "The flight is scheduled to depart from Terminal 1 at 1:15 PM. There's no way to check on this Magpie guy until I scan through all the check-in footage, which will take a while."

Noah glanced at his cell phone to see what time it was. Moore's plane left in less than three hours. Assuming he arrived early like most people did for international flights, it was possible he was already at the airport.

"Thanks, honey," Wes said before hanging up. "We owe you big."

While that was certainly true, Noah's mind was already a hundred miles away as he focused on how to find Peyton.

"There's no way in hell Moore will be able to get Peyton on board that plane with him," Lane said. "Which means either Magpie has her or they've left her somewhere else between here and the airport."

Noah's heart seized up in his chest. Lane had used a nice word for what they were all thinking. The truth was that if those assholes had left Peyton, it was because they'd killed her.

"Moore is our only link to Peyton," he said firmly. "No matter what, we have to stop him before he gets on that plane."

And hope she was still alive.

CHAPTER

PEYTON SQUEEZED HER EYES SHUT. CRAP, IT FELT LIKE someone was driving a spike into her head. She supposed that was what happened when someone slammed you into a wall. She couldn't believe Scott had betrayed her like that. She was sorry he'd gotten the shaft from the publisher, but that didn't give him the right to steal her book. Or kidnap her. Of course, she had a feeling that the other guy—the one actually responsible for her headache—was behind all of this.

She had to call Noah. Hopefully, he could stop the two men before they got away with her book.

Peyton opened her eyes slowly, ready to squint against the sunlight sure to be streaming through the windows into the apartment, but all she saw was darkness around her. For one terrifying moment, she thought the hit she'd taken had blinded her. No, she could see fine. It was dark.

Did that mean it was nighttime? Had she been unconscious all day? That was a terrifying thought all in itself. If she'd been out of it that long, why hadn't Noah found her and taken her to a hospital?

Peyton tried to roll onto her side and ended up hitting hit her head again. She automatically reached up to rub the offended area and discovered her wrists were bound together with something tight, thick, and sticky. It took her a couple of seconds of twisting and yanking to realize it was some kind of tape. She went to tear at the tape with her teeth, but that's when she realized she was gagged, too.

What the heck...?

She looked around the small space, able to see better now that her eyes had adjusted to the dim light. It took her less than a minute to figure out where she was, but when she finally did, her eyes went wide. She was in the trunk of a car. A car speeding down the road.

Crap, crap, and double crap!

Where the hell were Scott and Daris taking her? More importantly, what were they going to do with her when they reached wherever they were going? This was one of those moments when being a writer was a bad thing, because she had no problem coming up with all kinds of horrible scenarios about what they might have in store for her.

Peyton wiggled her wrists, struggling against the tape, but it was useless. She'd have to be Wonder Woman to tear the stuff. Then again, if she were Wonder Woman, she wouldn't be in this predicament. She would have kicked those guys' butts already.

If she got out of this, she was going to ask Noah to teach her some of his SEAL moves so she could defend herself in case some other crazy assistant editor tried to steal her book again and stuff her in the trunk of a car.

She stopped struggling against the tape, hope surging through her. If anyone could find her, it would be Noah.

Peyton tried to find solace in that while fighting back tears when the car suddenly slowed and turned before finally coming to a stop. From outside, she heard the distinctive echo of a plane taking off. It was still fading into the distance as the car door opened, then closed. She tensed as footsteps came around to the back of the vehicle. A moment later, the lid of the trunk opened.

Humid air rushed into the already blazing hot space, making it hard to breathe through the cloth stuffed in her mouth. She squinted against the brightness, lifting her bound hands to shield her eyes. Thankfully, Scott moved to block the sun. Daris stood a few feet behind him, completely uninterested in the entire situation.

Scott regarded her almost regretfully, his mouth pressed into a thin line. "I'm sorry we have to leave you in here, but we don't have a choice. When I get to Puerto Vallarta, I'll call the police and let them know where to find you."

Peyton's mind did a few quick calculations and realized Scott's plan would leave her trapped in this damn trunk for four to five hours...at least. She'd roast to death.

She started shouting against the gag in her mouth, cursing at Scott in between trying to tell him he didn't have to do this, that she wouldn't say anything to anyone. But with the gag in her mouth, all that came out was muffled noise. Not that it would have mattered. Scott slammed the trunk closed with a resounding thud, leaving her in darkness.

Tears burned her eyes again and this time she didn't try to hold them back. It was already over ninety-five degrees out today. The temperature inside the trunk of this car would easily reach a hundred and twenty. Sweat was already soaking her clothes and dripping off her face. She'd never make it until Scott reached Mexico and called someone.

Noah was going to have to find her soon or she was dead.

Noah left his SUV at the curb and raced into the airport, not giving a damn if the vehicle got towed. He didn't have time to dick around looking for a space in the parking lot. He had to find Moore and Magpie before the assholes went through security. If that happened, there was no way he'd ever reach them.

Behind him he heard the squawking of tires and knew Sam and the others had pulled up to the curb to help, but he had no intention of waiting around for them.

The airport was packed with people and

weaving his way through the maze was like navigating an obstacle course. All while looking for a needle in a haystack. He prayed he got lucky.

Scott Moore was nowhere to be seen around the Southwest check-in counters and Noah's stomach dropped. Cursing, he headed toward security. This was his last chance to stop the a-hole.

Please let there be long lines today.

Noah froze when he saw a man with blond hair standing in the line of people waiting to go through the TSA checkpoint. Noah couldn't see his face, but his gut told him it was Moore.

The guy turned to chat with the woman behind him. That's when Noah got a good look at his face and knew without a doubt it was Moore. Noah looked left and right but didn't see anyone that fit Magpie's description. For all he knew, Magpie might not even be here.

Noah slowly walked toward Moore. The last thing he wanted to do was spook the guy. Moore looked nervous enough already.

Noah moved casually as he walked along the security line, running through his options. If this were a SEAL mission, his plan of action would be simple. He'd pull his weapon and put a bullet in the guy's leg, then politely ask him exactly where he'd hidden Peyton. But doing that wasn't an option, not unless he wanted TSA all over him. Not to mention the uniformed cop who stood nearby. Something told Noah they wouldn't be interested in listening to his story.

He was still a few feet away from Moore when the man spotted him. The color drained from Moore's face, his eyes taking on a panicked look. He threw a quick glance at the TSA checkpoint, then at the exit door half a football field away. For a minute, Noah thought he might try to make a run for it, but instead, Moore darted out of line and slammed into the side of the unsuspecting cop.

What the hell was the man doing?

Then Noah saw him jerk the cop's gun from its holster and he knew exactly was Moore was doing.

Shit.

"Stay back!" Moore ordered, swinging the weapon back and forth between Noah, the cop, and the startled TSA agents. "Everyone stay back!"

Moore didn't need to tell anyone twice. All around Noah, frightened people screamed and ducked for cover. From the corner of his eye,

Noah saw Sam, Wes, and Lane, working to get people out of the danger area but there were so many people and most of them were frozen solid.

Noah held up his hands and stepped closer to Moore. He had his 9mm tucked firmly inside his waistband but adding another weapon in this situation wouldn't help. In fact, it would probably make everything worse.

"Take it easy, okay?" he said. "I don't care about the book. I just want to know where Peyton is."

The gun trembled in Moore's hands. "Peyton's fine. I'll call and tell you where she is after I get where I'm going."

Moore couldn't possibly be stupid enough to think the cops and TSA were going to let him get on a plane after this, was he?

Noah opened his mouth to urge Moore to put the gun down and tell him where Peyton was, but a sharp voice cut him off.

"Drop the gun and put your hands in the air! Now!"

Out of the corner or his eye, Noah saw a second cop had arrived and was aiming his weapon at Moore.

Shit, could this get any worse?

"Don't shoot him," Noah told the cop. "He kidnapped a woman and he's the only one who knows where she is."

The cop glanced at him sideways, then turned his attention back to Moore. "Put down the gun nice and slow and step away."

"Do as he says, Scott," Noah said. "It's the only way out of this."

Moore went back and forth between Noah and the cop, shaking his head.

The cop's finger tightened around the trigger. "I'm not going to tell you again."

Noah bit back a curse. If Moore didn't surrender soon, the cop was going to take him out. He wouldn't have any other choice. Noah tensed, ready to tackle Moore and wrestle the weapon from his hands when a gunshot rang out.

Moore crumpled to the floor, the gun sliding harmlessly out of his grip, blood staining the front of his shirt.

Noah was on the floor beside him in a flash. He gripped Moore's chin, turning his head so he could look at him. Moore gazed up at him in shock and confusion.

"Tell me where Peyton is," Noah urged.

"She's..."

Moore's voice was weak, and Noah had to lean close to hear him.

"She's in..."

"She's where?" Noah demanded.

Moore didn't answer.

Noah lifted his head to see Moore staring up at him with a blank look in his gray eyes. The stupid son of a bitch was dead.

Shit.

Noah got to his feet, fear like he'd never felt before gripping him. Around him, TSA agents and his SEAL teammates were trying to calm the gathered crowd even as the cop who'd killed Moore got on the radio to report what had happened.

How the hell was he supposed to find Peyton now? Scott was dead and none of them had a clue where Magpie was. Hell, Noah wasn't even sure if he'd know the man when he saw him.

Noah was just about to call Dwayne for his help when movement over by the TSA security checkpoint made him look that way. It took him a moment to figure out what had caught his attention, but then he saw the tall, dark-haired man stepping calmly through the full body scanner. Any other time, a person moving through security in an airport wouldn't have attracted notice. But any man walking this casually seconds after someone had been shot dead twenty feet away made you wonder what the hell was going on. The fact that the man matched the general description of Magpie was almost secondary at that point.

"Stop that man!" Noah shouted, pointing even as he took off in the same direction.

People started screaming, probably thinking someone else was going to start shooting, but Noah only had eyes for Magpie. The man was walking fast to get away, but with so many people freaking out, it wasn't like anyone noticed. Certainly not enough for somebody to stop the guy.

Noah jumped through the body scanner, intent on his target, when a uniformed cop stopped him.

"Freeze!" the cop shouted, his sidearm coming up even as more people began to scream and run. "Don't move."

Noah slid to a stop, cursing in frustration. Magpie—the only person who might know where Peyton might be—was getting away while a cop stood here slowing him down.

"The dark-haired guy who just went through security is an international terrorist," Noah said. "If he disappears, a woman could die!"

His announcement didn't faze the cop in the least, nor the other one that joined him, this one carrying a Taser. "Nice story, but if you take another step, my partner will tase you."

Noah caught sight of Magpie far away in the panicking crowd. The man turned and gave him a broad smile and a cavalier wave of the hand before disappearing from view. Cursing, Noah tensed, ready to take a swing at the first cop who got close to him.

He didn't get the chance.

Two figures came crashing through the body scanner, taking both cops down to the floor, disarming them at the same time.

"Go after him before he gets away!" Sam shouted, lying on top of the cop who'd been holding the Taser. "We'll give you time."

Noah glanced at Wes, who was pinning the other cop to the floor. There was no way in hell this didn't end badly for all of them. But he wasn't going to waste the sacrifice, even if it did end with him and everyone else going to jail.

He took off running, people climbing all over each other to get out of his way as he pushed and fought to get to the place where he'd seen Magpie disappear. When he got there, he skidded to a stop, cursing as he realized that the concourse branched off in two directions. Noah didn't pause to think. He simply turned right and kept running, praying for the best. People in this part of the terminal were far enough away from the insanity in the main concourse that they really had no clue what was going on, but they still stared at him running past them like a psycho. He ignored them and kept going. His knee throbbed with every step, but he ignored that, too, and forced himself to move even faster.

He reached the last gate at the end of the terminal without seeing anyone close to his target. His gut twisted into knots as he realized he must had taken the wrong direction and would have to backtrack and head toward the other end of the terminal. His heart plummeted when he saw more cops and TSA agents heading his way from that direction. There was no chance he'd be able to slip past them.

Then a dark-haired man came out of the restroom not ten feet away. *Magpie*.

For a moment, Noah considered drawing his 9mm, but instead, he lowered his shoulder and charged.

The guy barely had time to flinch before Noah slammed into him, tackling him to the ground.

Magpie grunted, the air rushing out, and Noah was sure that'd be the end of the fight. After all, Magpie was little more than a frigging glorified investment banker.

Turns out Noah was wrong.

Magpie slammed an elbow into the side of Noah's head, then slithered out from under him like a greased snake, moving so fast he was completely loose before the stars faded from Noah's vision. Then the man was on his feet, pulling Noah up to punch repeatedly at his throat, eyes, and groin, intent on killing or maiming him...in no particular order.

Noah fought back by pure instinct, blocking the worst of the blows with his forearms and thighs, getting in his own hits whenever he could. At the edges of his peripheral vision, he could see some people running while others pulled out their cell phones and recorded the fighting. He wanted to think there was something wrong with them, but that was simply how people were these days.

Another quick glance to the side revealed the cops and TSA agents closing in. Noah knew he had to finish this and get the answers to his questions about Peyton before the cops took that option away from him.

Noah blocked another ridge hand strike at his throat and countered with a right cross to Magpie's jaw. The punch should have staggered the man, at least momentarily, but Magpie barely blinked before moving in to drive his knee into Noah's balls.

Noah twisted, getting his left leg up in time to block the attack that would have dropped him for sure. On the downside, Magpie's shot caught him on the side of his injured knee and the pain he felt drove the air from his lungs and darkened his vision.

Shit.

He had to end this fight—now.

Getting his hands on Magpie's shoulders, Noah smashed his forehead into the bridge of the man's nose. Magpie began to slide to the floor and Noah was more than happy to let him fall, but the man clung to him. Noah thought he was trying to hold himself up, but then he realized what Magpie was doing and he cursed.

"He's got a gun!"

"Don't shoot!" Noah shouted, saying the first thing that entered his mind as Magpie backed away, Noah's 9mm in his hand. "He's got information vital to national security!"

For a fraction of a second, Noah thought that might stop the cops from taking out Magpie, but then three shots rang out.

Noah lunged for Magpie as the man went down. There was almost no chance the man was alive, not after getting hit three times. But the only wound Noah could see was at the man's shoulder. One hit out of three shots. Thank God for poor aim. But while the wound didn't look fatal, it was definitely bleeding heavily.

"Where's Peyton?" he demanded, getting a grip in Magpie's hair and giving him a rough shake as one of the cops slipped in to kick the 9mm aside. "Where is she?"

Magpie laughed, his eye starting to go blurry. "There's no way I'm telling you anything, other than to promise you'll never find her in time."

"Damn you! Talk to me!" Noah shouted, shaking Magpie again, but it was already too late. The asshole had fallen into unconsciousness.

An older cop with sergeant stripes on his sleeve was at his side, pulling Noah away as another began to apply first-aid to the injured man.

"Who the hell are you? Who the hell is he? And what the hell is going on here?" the cop asked.

"My name is Noah Bradley. I'm a Navy

SEAL." He ran his hand through his hair. "The guy bleeding on the floor is an international terrorist known as Magpie. He kidnapped Peyton Matthews this morning. Three members of my SEAL Team and I tracked him to the airport, hoping to find out where he left her. You can confirm the terrorist part of this story with Agent Glenn Woods from the Treasury Department at the San Diego field office."

The cop regarded him with a frown. "Peyton Matthews, the famous writer? She's been kidnapped by terrorists?"

Noah wanted to be surprised that a man as old as the cop ncw who Peyton was, but at this point, he was too wrung out to be surprised by anything. "Yes, and if Magpie's last words before he passed out are true, then we don't have much time to find her."

The cop shook his head. "I'm gonna have to call this in to my captain so we can get the feds involved."

The officer turned to walk away, pulling out his cell phone and probably starting a long chain of calls that would take hours to get anything done. Hours they didn't have. A few of the other cops looked Noah's way, but must have decided if their sergeant was going to ignore him, they would, too.

Noah dug out his phone, trying to figure out who to call—Woods, Chasen, or Dwayne. He was about to bring up his contact list when he an app icon caught his eye. It was the Find My Phone app Peyton had put on there. He was still staring at the icon when Lane walked up.

It couldn't be this easy, could it? Would Moore and Magpie have let Peyton keep her phone? It seemed too impossible to even consider, but still...

He clicked on the icon and connected to the sight—thankfully, Peyton's username and password were already filled in or this would never have worked—then waited impatiently for the app to locate her phone. If it said it was at his apartment, he was screwed.

But the app didn't point to his apartment. When the map screen first showed up, it was a wide angle shot of the city, then narrowed down until it showed a little red dot...at the San Diego International Airport.

He resisted the urge to let out a hooyah. Moore could have taken her phone and tossed it into a trash can when he got here, Noah thought as the map continued to zoom in. But when the red spot ended up in the middle of long-term parking, he knew he had something.

Hooyah.

Turning on his heel, Noah was ready to take off running back down the terminal until he saw the twenty or so cops and TSA agents standing between him and where he needed to go. And none of them looked like they were interested in letting him walk out of here.

"I hate to do this, but I need to get out of here—as in five minutes ago," Noah said, turning back to his Teammate. "Can you distract those cops?"

Lane looked over Noah's shoulder, then gave him a grin. "No problem."

Without another word, Lane jogged toward the cluster of cops, waving for them to follow him toward the connecting terminal. "I saw some more terrorists this way!"

While everyone else dived for cover, the cops and TSA agents took off running after Lane. Crap, he was going to be in so much trouble once everyone found out there were no more terrorists. But once again, Noah wasn't going to waste the sacrifice.

Noah ran through the terminal and into

the main concourse, then out the doors toward long-term parking. He'd never used the Find My Phone app before and he ended up running past the right location by a dozen feet or so before realizing he needed to turn around. Stopping, he scanned the area, taking in the dozen or so vehicles around him. He immediately discounted the pickup truck and minivan and instead focused on the obvious rental cars.

He pounded frantically on the trunk of each of them with his fist, calling Peyton's name, then pressing his ear to the lid to see if he heard anything in reply. He muttered a curse after the fourth car. It had to be close to a hundred degrees out here. With the sun beating down like it was, the trunk would feel like a frigging oven.

He banged on the fifth car, calling Peyton's name, then putting his ear to the lid. Instead of silence, this time he heard a muffled sound. His heart beat faster in his chest. He'd found her—and she was alive.

"Hang on!" he called. "I'm going to get you out of there."

Running around to the side of the car, he rammed the window with his elbow. The jacket he'd put on to hide the gun he'd been carrying protected his arm from the glass, and he quickly reached in to open the door. Not every car had a way to unlock the trunk from the inside, but he hoped this particular make and model might.

It didn't.

Shit.

Why the hell hadn't he thought to search Moore's pockets for the keys?

Noah stood and spun around, looking at all the other nearby vehicles. He saw exactly what he was looking for about five rows away—a beat-up old pickup truck with primer spots and a bunch of fish decals in the back window. That's what he needed—a truck that bellowed of a good ol' boy.

He sprinted over to the truck and looked in the back, finding pretty much what one would expect to see in the back of a truck that spent a lot of time in the woods and frequently needed working on. There was a spare tire, a rusted tool box, some lumber, tow ropes, jumper cables, and a shovel.

Grabbing the shovel, he raced back to the rental car Peyton was trapped in. He shoved the tip under the lid of the trunk, right where the latch was located, and yanked up.

The first time didn't work completely, but wedged the trunk open enough so he could jam it in a little further. Shoving hard, he popped the latch of the trunk open with a loud cracking sound. He tossed the tool aside, then quickly lifted up the lid.

Peyton blinked up at him from the small trunk space, breathing hard, tears in her eyes and her hair and clothes soaked in sweat. One look at her made Noah want to kill Moore all over again.

Slipping one arm around her shoulders and the other under her legs, he lifted her out of the trunk and gently set her on her feet. He quickly loosened the knot in the ugly tie Moore had used to gag her with, then went to work on the duct tape around her wrists. That took a little longer because he had to be careful not to hurt her, but as soon as she was free, Peyton threw her arms around him and hugged him tightly. He hugged her back, smoothing her wet hair with his hand and pressing a kiss to her head.

"You came for me," she said against his chest.

"I'll always come for you," he murmured.

"But how did you find me?" she asked softly.

"The Find My Phone app."

She pulled away enough to look up at him in confusion. "No, I meant how did you even know Scott and Daris had grabbed me?"

"Oh." He ran a finger down her cheek, wiping away a tear. "I was with Dwayne when the men who tried to kidnap you last night told him some big city guy who liked to twirl his pen all the time had hired them. I immediately knew it was Moore, especially since I thought he was a jackass the moment I met him. When I went back to the apartment and found the door open, the coffee mugs on the floor in the living room, and you gone, I figured Moore and the other guy had taken you with him. I didn't know his name was Daris. The U.S. government has been after him for a while, but they call him Magpie."

She shuddered. "Scott said he was taking a flight to Mexico. If we hurry, we might be able to stop him."

Noah gave her a wry smile. "The cops already took care of that. He's dead. And Magpie—Daris—has been arrested."

She looked shocked for a moment, then nodded. "I'm guessing they'll find a copy of my book in their luggage, if not on them. Whenever they get around to looking for it."

"We'll tell them in a little bit, but it might take a while to get it out of police and TSA custody."

She nodded. "It doesn't matter. It was a copy.

They left my hard drive at your place, so unless someone has messed with it, I'm fine. On the bright side, I did have a lot of time to think about a more dramatic way to end the story while I was lying in that oven of a trunk. I think the readers are really going to like it."

Noah pulled her close and hugged her again. "Has anyone ever mentioned you writers are crazy?"

She laughed and melted into his arms—exactly where he wanted her.

CHAPTER *Sixteen*

PEYTON LAY BACK WITH A CONTENTED SIGH, SMILING AS the sea breeze played with her hair. She'd finished her book and sent it off to Gwen that morning. To celebrate, she and Noah had invited some friends over for an impromptu party so they could all hang out on the beach and enjoy the ocean view.

Well, she supposed that everyone else was focused on the water. Peyton was more interested in how good Noah looked in those tight Navy-issue swim trunks as he walked out of the ocean to join her and the others in the chairs they'd sat up on the sand. It was damn near impossible not to stare at him. He could put a Roman statue to shame.

What? It wasn't her fault she couldn't stop looking at him.

"How did your medical exam go this morning?" Wes asked as Noah sat down in the chair closest to Peyton, groaning as the mid-day sun began to warm him up.

"Doc says my knee is responding well to physical therapy," Noah said with a grin. "And the MRI shows the tear that was there is well on its way to healing. If I don't do anything stupid for the rest of my medical leave, I should be back to a hundred percent in another three or four weeks."

Peyton wasn't sure if she was relieved or disappointed by Noah's announcement. While she obviously wanted his knee to get better, they'd talked enough to know once it was, he'd be going back to active status with his Team. That meant deployments and missions.

She took a deep breath and forced herself to relax. She was ready for this. With Noah's patience and understanding, trust in him and his Teammates, and the support of their friends, she'd be able to handle this. For a life with Noah, she could put up with anything.

"What about your career? Is that still intact, too?" Lane asked from where he sat nearby. "Has Chasen forgiven you for lying to him about everything?"

To say that Chasen was upset when he'd shown up at the airport and found Noah, Sam, Lane, and Wes being detained by the police was an understatement. The list of charges Noah and his friends had been facing was terrifying, not the least of which were assault on a police officer, resisting arrest, and bringing a firearm into an airport. In the end, an agent from the Treasury Department had shown up and made all the charges go away. But that still hadn't made Chasen happy. He'd been more pissed about Noah and the other guys not coming to him with the truth than he was about breaking the law. Peyton was pretty sure Noah was more hurt by his chief's disappointment than he'd ever been by the prison term the cops had threatened him with.

"We've talked about why I kept the truth from him," Noah said, grabbing a bottle of beer from the cooler that was within arm's reach. "I think he understands that I was just trying to protect him. He hasn't forgiven me completely yet, but we're getting there."

While Sam and Wes suggested ways Noah might get back in their boss's good graces, Lane chatted with Laurissa as Tabitha shyly flirted with another member of Noah's Team named Cade.

Peyton had only met him today, but he seemed very intrigued by Tabitha.

"Man, this is the life," Lane murmured, leaning back in his chair and staring out at the rolling ocean. "I would love to be able to walk out the back door of my apartment to a view like this every morning. I mean, your apartment is nice, Noah, but I can't imagine how you can go back there after spending time at a place like this."

Noah looked at Peyton. "Should we tell them?"

"Tell us what?" Lane asked.

Noah grinned and reached for her hand, interlacing his fingers with hers. "Peyton has asked me to move in with her and I agreed. I'm over here every night as it is. Like you said, it's a few steps up from my apartment. And the company is definitely a plus."

Peyton laughed, her heart doing a little dance in her chest. She remembered that conversation as if they'd had it five minutes ago. Not so much because she'd suggested him moving in, but because it was the first time Noah said he loved her.

It had come out casually while they were in her workout room during the middle of one of her yoga routines and his physical therapy sessions. She'd glanced over to see Noah gazing at her with this kind of dazed expression on his face, not doing anything but watching her. When she asked if everything was okay, he'd walked over and kissed her.

"I think I've known this from the moment I realized you'd been kidnapped," he whispered against her lips. "But for some reason, it really hit me right this second."

"What did?" she murmured, not sure where he was going.

"That I love you and can't imagine trying to live my life without you."

Her heart had done that same happy dance it was doing now, and it was all she could do to whisper that she loved him, too, and had since he'd found her in the trunk of that car. Exercise forgotten, they'd made love for the next two hours right there on the yoga mats.

"Have you told the rental office about dropping the lease on your apartment yet?" Sam asked, pulling Peyton out of her thoughts and back to the present.

"Not yet," Noah said. "I wanted to wait until I moved my stuff out first. Why do you ask?"

Sam shrugged. "I was thinking maybe I could

go with you and see if they'd let me sign a lease for your apartment right on the spot."

Peyton smiled, knowing how excited Sam was to finally be moving out of the barracks. He'd mentioned how much he hated living there at least a dozen times.

It was well after dark by the time the party wound down, and while Peyton loved hanging out with everyone, she was finally glad to have Noah all to herself.

"You know, I think my next book is going to be about a Navy SEAL," she said as they walked hand-in-hand down the moonlit beach, the warm water coming up to cover their bare toes.

"Seriously?" Noah glanced at her. "You think women would honestly want to read about a bunch of guys who do a crazy job for a living?"

She smiled. "I know they would. Navy SEALs are very popular right now."

"Huh," was all he said. "Who'd have thunk it?"

"You and your Teammates are heroes, Noah. And women love reading about heroes. Me especially." Peyton squeezed his hand. "Speaking of being my hero, I still can't believe you found me in that car at the airport that day."

It had been more than three weeks since

Scott and Daris had kidnapped her and she still had nightmares about being in small spaces.

Stopping, Noah lifted her hand, pressing a kiss to the palm. "I would have done whatever it took to find you. I was so terrified I'd lose you, I would have done anything to get you back."

The words made her catch her breath and she felt warm all over. Going up on tiptoe, she kissed him long and slow on the mouth. "You're never going to lose me. That's a promise."

He arched a brow. "Oh, really?"

"Yep." She smiled. "I'm requesting you for my lifelong bodyguard."

Noah chuckled and kissed her again. "I think that's one assignment I'm going to enjoy."

I hope you enjoyed Noah and Peyton's story!

Sam Travers is the next SEAL to fall in love when he meets the girl next door, who's more than she appears to be!

Look for their book soon!

Sign up for Paige Tyler's New Releases mailing list and get a FREE copy of SEAL of HER DREAMS!

Visit to get started!
www.paigetylertheauthor.com/

Want more hunky Navy SEALs?

Check out the other books in the *SEALs of Coronado Series!*

SEAL for Her Protection
Strong Silent SEAL
Texas SEAL
Undercover SEAL
SEAL with a Past
SEAL to the Rescue
SEAL on a Mission
Bodyguard SEAL

paigetylertheauthor.com/books/#coronado

For more Military Heroes check out my SWAT, STAT, and X-OPS Series!

SWAT: Special Wolf Alpha Team

Hungry Like the Wolf

Wolf Trouble

In the Company of Wolves

To Love a Wolf

Wolf Unleashed

Wolf Hunt

Wolf Hunger

Wolf Rising

Wolf Rebel

Wolf Untamed

Rogue Wolf

paigetylertheauthor.com/books/#wolf

STAT: Special Threat Assessment Team

Wolf Under Fire

Undercover Wolf

paigetylertheauthor.com/books/#stat

X-OPS

Her Perfect Mate

Her Lone Wolf

Her Wild Hero

Her Fierce Warrior

Her Rogue Alpha

Her True Match

Her Dark Half

Exposed

paigetylertheauthor.com/books/#ops

ABOUT PAIGE

Paige Tyler is a *New York Times* and *USA Today* Bestselling Author of sexy, romantic suspense and paranormal romance. She and her very own military hero (also known as her husband) live on the beautiful Florida coast with their adorable fur baby (also known as their dog). Paige graduated with a degree in education, but decided to pursue her passion and write books about hunky alpha males and the kick-butt heroines who fall in love with them.

She is represented by Courtney Miller-Callihan.

www.paigetylertheauthor.com

To be notified about Paige's new releases, get exclusive sneak peeks at upcoming books, deleted scenes, exclusive short stories, and giveaways, sign up for her newsletter. Your email will never be shared with anyone.

Sign Me Up!

paigetylertheauthor.com/subscribe

I'm excited to announce that I now have a FAN group on FB! It's a place to hang out with other fans—and me! Share stories and pictures, discuss what you love about my X-OPS, SWAT, Dallas Fire & Rescue, and SEALs of Coronado Series, as well as my other books!

And best of all, get sneak peeks before anyone else!

Hope to see you there!

www.facebook.com/groups/Paigetylersgroupies